MW01531031

The Day of the Dog

The feature film "Day of the Dog" is a Barron
Films Production. Made in association with
Australian Film Finance Corporation Pty Limited,
Australian Broadcasting Corporation and
Australian Film Commission.

Executive Producers: Paul D. Barron
                       Penny Chapman
Producer: David Rapsey
Director: James Ricketson
Screenplay: James Ricketson

Photos by Skip Watkins.
Front cover photo: John Moore as Doug
Dooligan.
Back cover photo top from left: John Hargreaves
as Detective Maxwell and John Moore as Doug
Dooligan.
Back cover photo bottom from left: Franklyn
Nannup as Roy, John Moore as Doug Dooligan
and David Ngoombujarra as Floyd Davies.

To Pa, Jane and D.A. Wallam

The Day of the Dog

Archie Weller

ALLEN & UNWIN
FICTION

© Archie Weller, 1981

This book is copyright under the Berne Convention.
All rights reserved. No reproduction without permission.

First published in 1981
Allen & Unwin Pty Ltd
8 Napier Street, North Sydney, NSW 2059 Australia

This edition published 1992

National Library of Australia
Cataloguing-in-Publication entry:

  Weller, Archie
  The Day of the Dog.
  ISBN 1 86373 241 1
  I. Title

Set in 11/13pt Garamond by Colset Pty. Ltd, Singapore
Printed by Australian Print Group, Maryborough

1

He's been drinking all day in the park, under the moulting trees that leave yellow tears strewn all over the scabby lawn.

The bubbly, noisy circle of nyoongahs has been visited by the police twice and the third time there will be some arrests for sure, because tempers are starting to warm up now after a day's drinking.

Everyone is celebrating Doug Dooligan's release from Fremantle jail after eighteen long, lonely months.

'Did ya see Uncle 'Erbie in there, Doug? 'E went in a couple months back for braining that old bastard down the Midland lockup.'

'Naw, Dougie would of been in New Division, or what?'

'Ow'd they treat ya, budda?'

'Poor ole Dougie. Garn, brother, 'ave a drink for me. I'm 'is own auntie, ya know.'

Words and leaves swirl around in the wind.

Doug gets drunk to forget those nights on lumpy beds in the overcrowded cells, with people keeping him awake pissing and shitting and dreaming out loud: to forget those days of milling around the yard or working in the garden — the same faces, the same walls, the same stories. In prison there is no privacy, no peace, nowhere to dream by yourself. That is what he missed most of all.

Now he can lie back and watch the cold, white sun slip in and out of heavy, grey clouds, elusive and cunning and always free.

It's going to rain soon. His first day out and it has to rain. Bloody typical.

Doug smiles to himself, lost in his own thoughts until a hand reaches inside his shirt and rubs his bony ribs.

'What ya doin' tonight, Dougie?' Jenny Campton whispers slyly.

He looks at her with bleary eyes. A couple of years ago, when she was sweet and fifteen, they were sort of going together. Now the fat rolls away from her eyes, her body and her hair are filthy and her breath smells. Besides, he hasn't got used to women yet after his absence.

'Gotta go home,' he manages to slur out and he staggers to his feet.

'Well, don't go yet, Doug. Stay and have a charge with us,' calls one old man, reluctant to see the money supply disappear.

'Doug's a bit under the weather,' cackles one young crone.

'Nuh, gotta go. See Mum.'

Yeah, well, look out for the monaych, budda.'

'Me and Willice'll see 'im to the bus stop. 'Ard luck if 'e goes back in, first day out,' a youth named Jerry grins, and two boys gather up the staggering skinny body that is so free, so drunk.

Three wobbling, untidy Aboriginal boys stumble along, heedless of the looks of distaste their journey provokes. As they cross the railway line, the unevenness of the ground becomes too much for Doug, who trips and falls heavily. The jolt sets his stomach in motion and he heaves upwards, retching and vomiting out all the flagons of wine and beer and the bottle of Coruba rum he has consumed; the rum he had promised himself the moment he was released.

Willice and his friend chuckle softly at Doug's misfortune then bend down to lift him up and gently wipe away all the mess from his face.

'Ya really buggered this time, Dougo. Too much gabba, what ya reckon?' Willice grins.

'Gi' me smoke, for fuck sakes,' mutters Doug.

'Train'll be 'long directly.'

'Fuck train. Fuck ever'body.'

He sits down again and shakily and ponderously rolls a cigarette, not caring about trains or rain or anything. Just being.

He grins up at his helpers' flat faces. 'Wha' you fink?' he gets out, then stops to light his smoke.

It won't light. He's too drunk and the weather's too windy. Willice's quick black fingers shelter the box and for a moment there is a brief orange flare before the match is dead and the cigarette alive.

Doug catches hold of the boy's arm and bursts into tears.

'Willice my bes' frien'. No-one love old Doug. No-one give a fuck,' he bursts out vehemently.

'Yeah, come on, buddy, before a train comes. Jerry, give us an 'and. Jesus, I didn't know Dougie could get so drunk.'

'Hey, y' know wha'? Guess wha'? Willice an' Jerry? I'm free, man. Free as fuckin' bird.' Doug shouts to the old buildings and the empty sky and to the empty people skittling past on the street. They see only the dusty and dirty outside of him, so they don't understand his joy. He waltzes around once then half staggers until the boys grab him again.

'Don' never go to jail, Will'ce. Fuckin' jail a bastard,' he says.

'Yeah, real bastard,' he muses before suddenly falling asleep on Willice's shoulder as is the way of drunks.

Willice and Jerry heave him over to a startled taxi driver, who almost cringes back when Jerry's dusky head thrusts through the front window. He would like to refuse the fare, but he does not dare unless he wants some rocks through his rear windows.

'Take our mate to Perth railway station, OK?'

'Listen, he's had it,' says the driver. 'He'll spew up all over my seat.'

'No 'e won't. 'E already did spew.'

The back door opens and Doug is pushed in, still sound asleep.

'He hasn't got any money. Look at him,' the driver complains, glancing at Jerry, who is young and fierce and who could be dangerous. Besides, he's still standing and able to throw a punch, whereas the potential passenger is harmless enough.

'Yes, 'e 'as got money, mate,' grins Willice. He, who is wise in the ways of the city, has taken off Doug's boot and extracted the fifty dollars hidden there. He keeps ten and gives ten to the driver.

'Remember, buddy,' smiles Jerry, 'we know you, so if we hear from Dougie ya never give 'im the right change, ya won't have no taxi left, will ya?'

He walks away with Willice.

The taxi pulls up outside the dark empty railway station and the driver shakes the thin, sprawled form awake.

'Here you are, mate. Here's your change back, too. Those two mates of yours took ten dollars for themselves.'

Eyes that can hardly open gaze at him uncomprehendingly and a mouth that will not close breathes wine fumes all over him.

'Huh. Yeah. Where fuck am I?'

'Perth.'

'Unna? But I was at Guildford . . .'

'Look, I have to go now,' says the driver. 'Bye.'

Doug staggers out of the taxi and it roars off. It's a Tuesday night, too, so the streets are almost empty and only the towering buildings seem alive with their flashing, blinking lights.

And when he came out, he had intended to walk these streets proudly, to get a job and show all the unbelievers what he really could be.

Perth has changed. For a moment he is afraid and huddles into a corner along with the spiders and old butts and other unwanted things.

Go for a walk and see if any acquaintances are around. But the few faces he sees are new or have changed to the point of being unrecognisable, as, no doubt, he has.

Things have certainly changed since he's been away. Where there was a traffic-bearing street, now there is a mall with seats and pot plants and a big stage in the middle. Doug climbs onto the wooden platform and does a waltz with an imaginary partner before he nearly falls off the edge.

On his way again.

New buildings are shooting up like grey toadstools. No lights for them yet, just hard, cement husks. Old buildings in the process of being torn down stand, defiant to the last, in their dusty rubble sea.

Everything has to go sooner or later. Old buildings, old people, old hopes.

He walks past a city hotel, with music from a wild band throbbing through the air and lights flashing golden-yellow behind the tinted glass.

Standing outside in the twilight, with the rain beginning to send short, stabbing spears into his miserable body, he has never felt lonelier.

Two forms hurtle out the door and cannon into him, sending him reeling.

'Watch who you're pushing into, mate. I'll knock you arse-up next time,' a gravelly voice snarls.

At the same time the other youth cries 'Look 'oo it is, will ya, Silver? Bloody Dougo.'

Brown hands steady the confused youth. He sees his two best friends of past days.

Silver's proper name is Sylvester Jackson. Once his mother must have had fine ideas for her only son. But he turned into a street person early in life, and the streets are a cruel and bitter place in which to grow up, for they love no-one; only the lights and the spiders and the rain and the sun. The streets gather up all the rubbish and all the stories and keep them close to their stony hearts forever.

Whereas Floyd Davey is quiet and sly, soft-footed and shy sometimes, Silver is loud and brutal. He has long, curly red hair, not quite in an Afro style and deep blue eyes that gaze into people, like a police car's headlights. He has tattoos all up his arms and over his back and chest, mostly showing naked women with proportions such as can only be dreamed of. At seventeen he is the youngest of the gang, yet he has a record longer even than

Floyd's. He is short, but very stocky, and quite willing to use his muscles. He is not clever, though, and never thinks before he acts; not like Floyd, who is as cunning as an old dingo.

Floyd, who is also called Pretty Boy, gives his easy smile and chuckles softly while he brushes Doug down and looks him over. As usual he is dressed neatly. He is wearing tight black jeans, a purple shirt and a denim coat. He is tall and loose-boned, a striking figure beside his paler tribesman, who slumps even further into his shabby clothes as the light leaps nimbly over his face.

'Ya one real mess, Dougo. We gotta get ya fixed up nicely for all the orgas, unna?'

'When did you get out, Dougo? I thought you were detained until the Governor's pleasure,' chimes in Silver, displaying his knowledge of legal terms.

'Well, come on, Silver,' says Floyd, we gotta 'ave a charge to celebrate our brother's release, or what.'

Floyd's arm wraps around Doug's shoulders and he drags him down a black and sinister alley that twists like a snake between tatty, old buildings. This alley is an old friend. Here, many times, they have all sipped sensuous bitter wine and giggled out their little stories of life. Here, at the back of the YMCA, Doug had committed his first crime. He and Floyd stole five hundred dollars' worth of travellers' cheques from an old drunk, temporary, resident of the YMCA and Doug forged the old man's name to get all the money. They bought new clothes and cowboy boots for themselves and a new broom and lots of groceries for Floyd's Mum. They spent the weekend playing pool, handing out money and getting drunk until a jealous rival dobbed Floyd in. The CIB plucked him from the company of several admiring girls when he was rotten drunk. They found a hundred dollars still on him as well as a ring he stole two weeks before and which he was saving up for some special girl when she came along.

So Floyd went to Hilston, from which he soon ran away. Although the detectives flogged him, he did not tell them the name of his accomplice, so Doug went free that time.

That episode was the start of Doug Dooligan's underworld

career. Now he has a record and a sentence to prove that he is what everyone said he would be.

He isn't much to look at, really. He is not tall like Floyd or solid like Silver; he is thin, forlorn and shabby.

Eighteen months in prison have given him shifty, downcast eyes, a sullen mouth and hunched shoulders. His head is pushed down so he looks like a vulture on a tree watching dinner crawl by. His grey cat eyes are always alert except when he is drunk or hiding something. Russet hair falls in disorganised tangles about his face. Once he had long, wavy hair that was the envy of everyone. It used to shine, gold and alive, in the disco lights and the city lights, and every girl wanted to run her fingers through the fine strands.

But they cut it all off in prison and he has given up trying to keep it tidy. No girls came to see him in prison; only his sister and mother sometimes.

Now Doug, Silver and Floyd emerge from the alley mouth onto the street, the two Aboriginals holding each other up, and the white youth, Silver, just far enough behind to prove to them that he is a friend and to anybody else that he is not that much of a friend, really.

'What about this drink, then? Could do with a drink,' grunts Silver. His eyes flicker around for signs of trouble or easy women — the two most common factors in his life.

Floyd grins at Doug.

'Where's all ya boya, brother? Bet ya got paid plenty for one and a half years, unna? We'll go and pick up a woman for ya, Dougo. Would ya like a big fat wadgula or a skinny little gin?'

'What about that Chinese woman? She was A one, man,' Silver joins in.

'Nah. We'll get Dougo a proper moony. Poor bugger, never seen 'ide nor 'air of a woman for two years nearly, ain't it, budda?'

'Is that going to worry Doug; no women being there? I thought his true form would come to light,' teases Silver.

Floyd leans close to Doug and asks, 'So where's all that lovely money, my brother?' He winks at Silver, who grins back.

'Well, I dunno,' Doug stammers. 'I . . . I gotta get 'ome. See Mum. Bin out since this mornin' and 'aven't seen 'er yet.'

'Your Mum doesn't want to see you, Doug. You may as well be dead for all she cares. Where you bin all day, then?'

'I was down Lockridge camp when I come out,' Doug says.

'What ya go and visit them bludgers for? They never come to visit you in jail,' Floyd points out, brusquely.

'Neither did you, either.' Doug suddenly remembers and slips out of the loving grasp around his shoulders and the quick-fingered grasp in his pockets.

'Ya never one time come to see me and I got you out of all sort of shit, 'fore I went in. Ya don't give a fuck for me, Pretty Boy. And Silver too, ya white cunt. What am I doin' with you mob, anyways? Ya fuckin' criminals an' I'm s'posed to not see youse, so up ya bum.'

Then a police patrol materialises out of the alley.

'What's going on?' says the taller of the two policemen, staring at the angry Doug and his two grinning companions with hard eyes.

'Oh, just me mate letting off steam, sir. He only come out of jail today.' Floyd smiles, while Doug hangs his head and shuffles his boots at the sight of the dreaded uniform.

'OK fellahs, you'd better get him home before he does more than use abusive language,' says the policeman.

'Right-oh,' agrees Floyd.

The two men wander away up the street.

Floyd's smile disappears. He drags Doug into the shadows underneath the scaffolding of yet another dying building.

'Listen, Dougo. We never come to see ya in jail because Freo drives us crazy.'

'Ya never bin there, so what'd *you* know?' Doug growls.

Silver closes up on the other side and smiles mirthlessly.

'Pretty Boy, looks like your Dougo got some teeth.'

'Ya owe me ten dollars from before ya went in, Dougo, so if ya gunna be poxy and not drink with ya old mates, all right. But you give me that ten dollars now or I'll bust ya fuckin' 'ead in,' Floyd murmurs. And Doug remembers that the softer Floyd's voice becomes, the more violent and dangerous his temper.

'Yeah, well, I was only jokin',' he mutters. 'Course I'll drink with ya.'

An arm wraps around him and Floyd smiles again.

'Let's go before the pubs close,' he says.

Doug is truly back home now, back to his old style, and he hasn't even been out a day. He told the prison superintendent, the psychologist lady with the frightening eyes and all his cell-mates that he would never go back there.

Yet here he is with the two people he said he wouldn't see. What will happen if Floyd steals a car and they get caught, or if Silver gets in a brawl — or even if he himself gets in a brawl again like last time?

Now they are going through the doors of the hotel. The loud music, happy laughter and voices deafen him whilst the flickering seductive lights that flirt with the shadows, blind him. He just doesn't care any more.

They drink up all Doug's money, then Floyd pulls out some of his own and Silver mysteriously discovers a ten dollar note in one of his pockets. During the evening, three Aboriginal girls come in and move swiftly over to the youths' corner. The tall, honey-brown youth slaps Doug genially on the shoulder and pokes out his long, pink tongue, saying proudly 'Look 'ere Dougo, this 'eres my woman Valerie, and these two minnies is 'er cousin and sister. 'Told ya I'd get ya one woman,' he shouts above the music before dragging his giggling girl out onto the floor to dance.

The music is too loud for Doug to talk in his prison-muted voice. Once or twice he glances at his companion, then lets his eyes slip back into the golden-hearted world of his beer.

Soon it's one o'clock in the morning.

Day over. Disco over. Time to go home.

Floyd and Silver support a sagging, gagging Doug, who is sick again. Their three girls walk behind them.

The youths sing and laugh, all mates together; all drunk

together. Just like that other night when Doug had the fight that resulted in his being put away.

Floyd does steal a car; a yellow Monaro parked outside a flash nightclub that he knows he will never enter. So he steals the car, his fingers as dark as night clouds and a sly smile on his purple lips.

He and Silver push Doug into the back and the smallest of the girls squeezes beside him, hoping she might get a bit of a kiss and a cuddle even though she missed out on a dance.

Doug looks at her and sees a young teenager with bright eyes peeping from below her untidy blonde fringe. She's not even fifteen, but that's the way it goes.

'Oo are you, any rate, bud?' She asks him. 'Never seen you around before.'

'I come out of prison just today.'

'Unna? I bet you was in for *murder*,' she exclaims.

'Nuh. I just 'ad a fight, is all.'

A little arm wraps tentatively around Doug's shoulder and she moves closer to him. This is better than going with one of those loud-mouthed boys who tramp the streets, who shout and catcall and dance out stories to the electronics and bells of the pinball machines, who grab a girl and pull her into a corner to kiss and cuddle, fondle and hit, then take home to bed.

'What's ya name, anyway?' she asks Doug.

Silver stops necking with his latest conquest to grin over into the back seat.

'*He's* Ned Kelly, Sunshine, so look out he doesn't shoot you with his gun,' he says.

Floyd, one arm around the wheel of the car he loves and one around the girl he thinks he loves, laughs loudly as the car squeals around a corner.

'Get on to 'er, Dougo. Ya got the 'ole back seat for yaself, there.'

Doug focuses on the girl again. In a ragged way she *is* pretty. Certainly a better proposition than battered, fat, yellowtoothed Jenny Campton. It has been a long time since he has had a woman

10

except in his dreams, so he leans close to her ear and whispers.

'Ya wanna go with drunk old Doug the thug, or what?'

She giggles her answer before her swift tongue darts into his mouth.

Doug is in a world of his own, drunk on alcohol and love, drunk on being free and hurtling down the road of life once again.

Floyd is currently staying in a block of flats; the police don't yet know his address. It's a square and solid building, set in a neatly mowed lake of grass with demure young gum trees all around.

Silver, Doug and the girls scramble out while Floyd drives off to ditch the car somewhere. They huddle under a tree and try to keep warm by kissing and squeezing and thinking of the night to come. Floyd's woman smokes a cigarette.

Then the grinning Floyd struts out from the shadows and they troop upstairs to his place.

Floyd's woman Valerie lives there, really, but whatever she has automatically become Floyd's property.

It's a nice, clean place. Floyd makes sure of that. There are two holes in one door and one in another: Floyd's trademarks. When he gets drunk sometimes, he flies into sudden rages, smashing anything or anyone who gets in his way, there is no stopping him, but right now he is like a sleek, well-fed panther, content with life. Now he pads softly into the kitchen and soon reappears with a huge grin and a big bottle of whisky.

'Da dah!' he shouts, with a flourish.

'What are you wastin' that for?' sulks Silver.

Floyd flops down beside his woman.

'This is for Dougo's release, see,' he explains. 'E's me mate, ain't it, Dougo? Ole uncle Floyd'll look after ya, good way.'

'Doug's 'ad enough to drink,' Silver sneers.

Doug certainly has. It is taking all his strength to keep his eyes open and to hold onto his new little love. At last he gives up and falls asleep, an arm around her waist and his head on her narrow shoulder. In his dreaming he is safe and warm once again, so a gentle smile drifts onto his thin, confused face.

Floyd's eyes go dark and he mutters. 'Well, *I'll* drink it, then.

'Oo stole it, any rate? Not *you*, you shifty-arse bastard.'

So Silver shuts up and concentrates on his girl. Soon they get up and stumble into the bedroom. Floyd moodily sips his whisky, feeling as lonely as the moon.

'Ya picked a right ole one for me sister, Pretty Boy. 'E can't 'ardly stand up,' giggles Valerie.

'Nana will look after 'im, unna, Nana?' Floyd smiles and takes a thoughtful gulp of whisky while Doug's girl nods nervously.

'Poor ole Dougie. I never know'd 'e 'ad such a temper before that fight,' he tells Valerie. He hauls her off to bed, leaving Doug and his girl alone.

Her name is Polly. She is the sister of Floyd's girl Valerie, and the cousin of Silver's girl Rebecca. Like most Aboriginal girls of her age she is 'on the run' from the Community Welfare Department and she supposes one day they will catch her but she makes no real attempt to hide.

Her life is like that of a bumble-bee stopping to sip nectar here and there, then on again, but always ending up back in the hive. At the age of three she was taken from her sad, drunken wreck of a mother and placed in Sister Kate's home where she remained with a kindly cottage mother for two years before being reclaimed by a grandmother influenced in part by vague feelings of affection but even more by a desire to claim the child endowment.

After that there was a spell back with her mother until she was returned to Sister Kate's, this time accompanied by several of her numerous brothers and sisters. The pattern was repeated until by the time she was twelve and surviving by rolling old drunk white men and other such activities she graduated to Nyandi Correction Centre. She ran away and from then on her existence has been one of escape and recapture by the Department.

Her own mother barely remembers her now. Soon she will become a mother herself — and the whole cycle will start again.

Small wonder that her philosophy is to squeeze as much fun out of life as she can while she can and not plan for the future.

Love holds no secrets for her. Three years ago, when she was only twelve, some forgotten man broke her in and went on his way. Her life since then has been full of similar experiences; she has never really enjoyed them, but she knows what love is. All it means is to open her legs and to twist in sordid mechanical motion until the man has had his fill of her, then roll over and forget about him as he forgets her.

But Doug has caught her attention. Tonight at the disco, she has watched him get drunk and has seen in his strange, grey eyes a sadness that prison has not given him; something that lurks in the background, asking to be caught yet never giving anyone a chance. Doug's thin lips hide a sensitivity that she cannot understand, yet she knows that he is a gentle person. He will not hurt her as Floyd is apt to hurt his woman at any drunken moment and crazy Silver will do at any time.

She runs a finger over his craggy face and gently nibbles his ear so that he murmurs in his sleep.

Polly wonders what he is dreaming about. Jail, perhaps? And what did he fight over, so that they sent him there? She imagines what it will be like to go with this thin, sad youth.

She gently pushes him down on the couch and finds a blanket, then snuggles up close to him, for it is May now and the nights are cold.

2

Doug is so accustomed to being roused by the jangling of keys and the shouting of warders at seven o'clock that he wakes early, hung over though he is. He awakens suddenly, not hearing any noise and wondering if he has slept in and will be late for morning parade. He forgets where he is for a moment and stares in stupefaction at the softly snoring girl close to him on the cramped sofa.

If he moves he will disturb her and he doesn't want to do that yet. She looks exquisite with her smooth honey-brown skin and her moist lips that inspire all kinds of delightful thoughts in him. Her long eyelashes brush her cheeks. A black orchid would be no lovelier.

He seems to remember kissing her last night, but everything about last night is just a great stew of familiar and strange faces, voices and music.

So he lies there and watches the sun slink into the cold, dark room like an unwanted guest. His eyes can see most of the room; not that there's much to see, really.

The room has two chairs, the couch, a television set and a table. There are ornaments; and just a few photographs of babies on the wall.

There would always be husbands drunk and brothers gambling and sons in jail and fighting and swearing and everyone giving up. But, as long as there were babies to hold and love, hope would be reborn all over again and there was something worth living for.

The babies smile down at Doug, their optimism captured forever by the photographer's bulb.

He turns his head and sees the girl smiling at him.

'Well, 'ullo. What 'appened last night?' he asks her.

'You was really drunk, Dougie. Floyd and Silver brought ya 'ome 'ere. My sister owns this flat, see, and we all live 'ere together. Floyd stole one nice Monaro. Could 'e make it move, or what?' She grins, hugs Doug close to her and whispers, 'I reckon ya solid, Doug. Ya wanna go with me?'

'Why not?' he whispers back and hugs and kisses her properly.

How many times he has thought of this moment, of holding a woman again instead of cold, cruel phantom women or lumpy pillows during the dead nights he spent inside. In Freo there was no dancing, or brilliant lights, or golden and red bottles of beer and wine; no shouting at the moon in carefree joy or murmuring to the sun in happy, lazy appreciation. No silken, flowing, black hair and sweet perfume and clinging clothes and voices twittering like birds in a mulberry bush. There was just angry Micky Connelly, boss of the cells, who was in for rape and who used to grate out his various violent stories and Danny Forsyth, slim, dark and dangerous as a dugite, with mad eyes and a slash for a mouth that bled poison and hate. He was in for jumping all over a white boy after knocking him out with an iron bar, just for something to do on a boring Saturday night.

Doug thinks about Eddie Wundonie the fullblood boy from Mowanjum mission who came down to visit Perth and who teamed up with a city aboriginal. His mate stole a truck and they decided to drive up north back home to Eddies country. But the truck rolled over just out of Bullsbrook and when the roving police van found the two young men trying to hitchhike to Geraldton, they arrested them. At the police station, they made the mistake of treating Eddie Wundonie like a Perth boy. The Mowanjum youth, as proud and indestructible as his country, fought off almost the entire lockup staff before being subdued.

Eddie would laugh one moment and cry the next. He would dream and scream aloud at night and sing Mowanjum songs monotonously, not caring about Micky Connelly's huge muscles and Danny Forsyth's mad eyes. He would sing and will himself back to his country, out from the cold walls that tried to squeeze the pride from his sun-kissed and cyclone-caressed body.

Doug comes back to the present. Here there is just a pretty girl with soft, inviting lips and hips, and golden musky breasts hiding in the darkness and softness of her jacket.

Love on a Wednesday morning.

They struggle out of clothes and are tangled in the blanket. They giggle and whisper, kiss and explore. Grey eyes lock with warm brown eyes and they understand each other and each gives a part to the other so they are whole. In one sense both are in the same state of being; Polly temporarily free but glancing over her shoulder on the lookout for police or the Welfare, and Doug stumbling off down the road, free again.

Are they free?

No. He and she are both trapped in a lifestyle they can never escape. Might as well make the most of each other while they are together.

Afterwards they lie in a tangle of clothes and blanket and happy thoughts.

'I don't even know ya name, look', says Doug. 'Ow come you know mine?'

'Floyd told me. Anyway, my name's Polly.'

'Polly put the kettle on and we'll 'ave a cup of tea,' he grins.

'But everyone calls me Nana. You know, like in banana.'

'Funny, unna? I mean, first night out and I meet you and 'ere we are, all warm and snug as a bug in a rug.' He pauses as he recalls that that was one of his Dad's expressions.

When the mood was on him, Carey Dooligan would recite Banjo Patterson by the yard, usually in winter when the huge fire was alight and blazing a fierce red and all the work was done. With a good feed inside him and a glass of wine in his hand, Doug's Dad had been almost good.

16

'What ya thinkin' about?' the girl murmurs and presses against him. 'Ya do a lot of thinkin', Dougie. All last night I was watchin' ya. Real quiet, ya are. Too quiet.'

Silver bursts from the bedroom, half-naked and grotesque in his pallor, with his bright red hair sticking out everywhere as though it were flames and not hair at all. His blue eyes take in the scene and he cackles, so that Doug and Polly feel as though their little interlude is now something dirty and not pure childlike love any more.

'Yeah, Dougo. Typical sly old bastard *you* are. Wait till we've all gone to bed then a bit of how's your father, eh?'

Polly slips into her dress and goes into the kitchen.

'She's a bit of all right, isn't she, Doug?' Silver winks and pinches her bottom as she disappears. 'Swap you over tonight.'

Doug relaxes on the couch, lazy and easy. He smiles at Silver.

'No way, budda. She's mine.'

'Hah!' the white youth spits. 'Our Dougo's got himself tied down already and he hasn't even been out for a day.' He rolls, laughing, into the kitchen.

Doug closes his eyes again. He doesn't have to get up at some ungodly, miserable hour. He doesn't have to wander around and around the same small yard with two hundred other men all dressed the same, all with the same look of boredom, sullenness and not giving a shit, the worst atmosphere he has ever been in. He doesn't have to cut lawns and rake up debris and weed gardens and cut wood and so on and so on, all for hardly any money, under the watchful eye of a man who, deep down if not openly, scorns and mocks him. He doesn't . . . well . . . he just doesn't. He can lie here forever and he's with his friends and he has a woman whom he does like and who seems to like him.

That's what life's all about.

'Fuckin' beautiful,' he breathes, still dreaming.

'Ya never even tasted it yet,' comes Polly's murmur beside his ear. He opens his eyes to a dish full of fried egg and bacon. Silver, his mouth full of toast, mumbles gleefully.

'Jesus, Dougo, what have you got hidden away to warrant you

breakfast in bloody bed?' He perches on one of the chairs and grins at the pair.

'You like my new tattoo, Doug? It's of my old woman in there. He points, with a nod of his head, to the open bedroom door. The tattoo itself is of a huge-breasted Negro woman with a mean-looking snake wrapped around her middle.

'It's pretty,' Doug says.

'I got it for half price off Billy Todd. I give Billy this radio I nicked from a car,' Silver tells him proudly.

'Fuck stealing. I'm goin' straight from now on,' says Doug and decides to get up.

'Well, what ya come for a ride with us last night, then? That car was 'ot like Polly's dot,' comes Floyd's nasal voice from behind, so everyone jumps.

For all his height, which is a slim six foot one, if Pretty Boy Floyd doesn't want to be seen he won't be. If he does, he will suddenly float from nowhere like a ripple on a pool surface, and catch everyone unawares.

Now he grins amiably down at Doug and claps a slender hand on his shoulder.

'So 'ow ya keepin', ya big 'ole? Good to 'ave our brother with us again, unna, Silver?'

'Sure is,' the redhead grunts unenthusiastically.

Floyd drops into the remaining chair, rubs fingers into his sleepy eyes and scratches his long, molasses-dark hair.

'Give us a smoke, Polly,' he says and she lights him a cigarette.

They all share the smoke and talk while the sun fades and the rain clouds gather for their corroboree.

They talk about friends inside and outside: Yellow Joe, a half-Chinese youth, is in hospital after smashing up a stolen car during a high speed chase. Billy Moreton killed his young wife and then shot himself.

Riley Keeley, Floyd's cousin, has become a homosexual and was getting two hundred dollars a go from old midnight cowboys in the Hay Street mall.

Doug remembers Riley Keeley as a small gentle boy, with the

biggest eyes he has ever seen; brown and soft and warm, like a horse's. He was the referee when Doug and Floyd had their first fight. Floyd told Riley to smash Doug with a flagon if he fought dirty. That was a horrible night, with a reluctant, peaceful Doug letting Floyd vent his anger on him, then Doug trying to kill himself with the jagged end of a beer bottle. Little Riley took it from him, hugged him and led him home while Floyd bellowed like a bull, stabbing himself again and again in front of screaming, crying girls, for fighting with his best friend.

But they were young then and drunk on sweet cruel sherry.

Riley was there when Doug's dog was run over by a carload of white boys. Only he, of all the people there except Doug's mother, understood the boy's grief and shared in it. They buried the dog together and drank beer outside to forget.

Now Riley is ostracised by his people and society. Strange things happen to sensitive people who are locked up too soon, too long, too often. Riley's brother shut himself in his room for three long months when he came out of jail and hardly emerged except to get food and drink. He didn't associate with any of his friends from the small country town where the Keeleys live, but just played records all day. Riley, with his soft eyes and gentle nature, had been an easy victim for the depraved inhabitants of jail and had learned a profitable trade in there as a result.

Outside, the trees whip and snap in a wild, beautiful ballet with the wind, and shriek like the hounds of death. The rain clouds creep on purple bellies towards the horizon and hurl out thunderous war cries.

Outside it grows dark and cold, but inside it is warm with friendship and feeling.

They talk about who is living with whom and who has whose babies. Death and birth, love and hate, football and sex. Cigarettes. Valerie and Silver's girl Rebecca crawl out of bed about midday and add their giggles to the conversation. Doug tells of his experiences inside; those that aren't too private to tell any but his best friends, when they are alone. (Like the times he cried at night, or the time in the Juvenile Section, when he first went there, that he bashed his fists bloody, pounding at the unyielding, mocking wall.)

Floyd sends the girls to buy some chicken at the take-away and the boys watch television for a while.

But at last Doug has to face going home to his mother. Polly sees him sadly to the door.

'Will I see ya t'morrow, Dougie?' she asks.

'Course, baby,' he smiles and winks. 'Gotta see Mum, but. She gets worried and me parole officer might of rung up or something.'

Even now he isn't entirely free. Somewhere, in the background, lurks an aftercare officer or a parole officer, like Banquo's ghost, always ready to disrupt the banquet with truths from the past.

'Goodbye, then. I love ya, you know. Ya my man, unna?' she asks earnestly.

'Why not?' he smiles, then casually waves cheerio and sets off into the growing dark.

It starts to rain. The cool, grey fingers straighten out his hair so it hangs ragged around him, and bite into his skin while he waits at the bus stop. He digs his hands deep into his pockets and wishes he was back with Polly, listening to Silver and Pretty Boy laugh and joke. There he was someone, not just a part-coloured ex-criminal.

The wind has died down now and the trees stand dark and silent. Far off in the city, he can see lightning jabbing at the towering buildings and the buildings' black forms seem to leap at the sky's underbelly with each flash.

The bus eventually comes and he climbs on. He huddles up in the far corner of the green, rumbling, clanking monster, away from the eyes of the curious and the scornful; he buries himself deep into his coat and thinks of his mother.

3

The house is the same as it has always been; old and with an air of enchantment.

One of the first houses in this area of East Perth, it still has its shingle roof under the red painted corrugated iron and its back doorstep has been worn down by the countless feet of generations.

Still the same, silent and reproachful in the grey, lancing rain.

He clambers up the front steps then stands uncertainly as the wind whips his mongrel body and shrieks like a devil woman.

The last time he saw his mother was seven months ago, when she visited him in jail. Even then they didn't have much to say; they never have done.

He knocks on the front door, realising that it has been newly painted. He sniffs noisily and lights a cigarette before the door opens slowly and his mother's pale face peers out at him.

'Douglas?'

Force a smile and nonchalantly stuff his hands in his pockets.

'G'day, Mum. I just got released today,' he lies from behind his cigarette.

'Well, come on in.'

He follows her inside. Quiet and peace glide hand in hand through a different world. In the huge dining-cum-sitting-room are bookcases, soft chairs and a sofa that belonged to his grandparents. Weathered and dusty pictures peer down from every wall, welcoming him home. Inside the fireplace an electric heater beams cheerfully.

'Let me have a look at you, darling,' says his mother.

He turns and tries to stare into her brown eyes, but, like waves slipping off a rock, his own grey ones hide from the pain and honesty he sees there.

'You've most certainly changed, Douglas. You look a lot older.' She smiles wistfully. 'Perhaps wiser?'

Shrug his shoulders and chuckle uneasily. Clutch his little battered case tighter for it is the one thing he is sure of.

'Well, a cup of coffee? Do you like what I've done to the house? There's no need for so many rooms now that you're gone and Tom's . . .' She stops then puts on a false, bright smile. Can't hide the pain in her eyes, though.

Tom was her eldest child. He was intelligent, outgoing and so alive, with a cynical smile on his lips always ready with a quick, often cheeky answer.

His mother used to joke that he even came into the world arguing lustily about his rights, with a bellowing mouth and a red, angry face.

After Tom followed strawberry-blonde-haired Jemima and five years later as an afterthought, skinny, curly-haired Douglas appeared.

But Tom was always the favourite, until he grew to manhood and made it plain that there was no way he would stay on the five hundred acre property that Carey Dooligan had hacked out of the bush.

He went wandering, as all the Dooligan menfolk were apt to do. He grew his hair long and marched in peace marches. Words like 'hippy', 'Moratorium' and 'Vietnam' crept into young Doug's vocabulary. Despite the age difference, Tom always had time to talk to him and explain things; more time than his dour father, who was too busy with the land he loved and needed; more than his sister, who was twelve then and trying to be the little lady. Doug loved Tom with a child's whole hearted hero worship.

Doug hadn't understood his brother's ideas about war though. He and his mates used to play soldiers a lot down by the old water-hole. He understood that, for it was fun, and fun is what it's all about when you're only seven.

But then his brother was called up. They cut off his hair and put him in a green uniform. They gave him a gun and told him to kill people. Tom, who loved life and talk and red wine on summer nights, who listened endlessly to Beethoven and Strauss, Chopin and Mozart, and revered beauty above everything else; who had never lost his temper in his whole short life.

A bomb smashed him against the sky a month after he was sent to Vietnam.

Doug never played soldiers with the kids again.

Now twelve years have passed and it is the beginning of a new decade and a new era. Doug's first tentative steps as a man have been taken, and he has stumbled. Jemima is married with children. Yet his mother has never forgotten her first-born.

'Yeah, well. What about a cuppa?' Doug touches her hesitantly, for he is not much of a touching person. But he brushes her shoulder so she won't cry, since tears are the last thing he wants now. 'I'll make it.' He wanders into the small kitchen, only it isn't a kitchen now but a store room.

'Tricked me,' he smiles.

'Oh, yes. The new kitchen is Dad's old office.'

'Righty-oh.'

He hums and watches the rain dribble down the window as the kettle whistles joyfully. Sometimes a raindrop slithers sensuously after another. If it catches up, they join together and, making violent love, they speed down the glass to dash against the wood.

He smiles at the thought and thinks of the morning and Polly.

Then the kettle is bubbling and he makes the coffee. He goes back into the dark, ornament-cluttered room, warm with artificial fire. Everything is artificial.

He holds the cup to warm his hands.

'I was thinkin' of Dad, out there,' he says. 'The way he used to sit behind his desk, like old Hanley, our principal at school, ya

23

know. I seen 'im one time. Yeah.'

'Oh?'

'Yeah. But I was in the Juvenile Section, so I couldn't talk to 'im. Well, 'e wasn't there long. In for drinkin' again, I s'pose; I dunno. They shipped 'im out to Wooroloo, I think, yeah.'

'Well,' he raises his eyes from the comforting blankness of the table into his mother's earnest stare. ''Ere's to a long life and an 'appy one,' he smiles.

'I certainly hope so,' is all she says.

They drink and she hopes he will tell her about jail, but he is silent. His grey eyes hold a wistful look and there is a hard stubbornness about his mouth that was not there when he was seventeen, with a dreamer's eyes and a romantic's lips and the laughter of a child born of the earth and the sky.

He hardly smiles any more, just lifts his lips faintly. Behind his eyes, secrets are locked up as securely as he himself had been every night.

'So you saw your father in prison?'

'Well, ya know what 'e's like,' Doug mumbles, thinking.

Carey Dooligan. His father. He hadn't seen him since he was fourteen and they had had to leave the farm.

Carey's father Tom was white, but his mother was a half-caste. However, old Tom had been good to her and his four brown children and gradually the district became used to seeing them as a family, although there was always whispered gossip about 'that Mary Dooligan'.

Doug can recall his grandmother as a wizened, quiet old woman who softly hummed hymns.

The two older Dooligan boys inherited a wanderlust from their mother's race and, as soon as they were old enough, they drifted out of the district. But the youngest son, Carey, stayed on to look after the little kingdom old Tom had founded.

The daughter, who had her mother's peaceful nature and her father's flaming hair and vitality, became pregnant to her cousin, the half-caste Dobie Greyboy and went off to Perth to start a new dynasty.

24

But Carey married Edith Menzies.

The Menzies had been in the district as long as the Dooligans. When the fathers of Edith and Carey had been young men, they were the best of friends. They were next door neighbours and often helped each other out.

John Menzies was a dour Presbyterian who saved all his money and was able to give his three daughters a good education. He was one of the first in the district to have a car. He would light his pipe in front of the huge fire at night, and remark to his wife that all was right with the world.

Then, suddenly, all was not right. Out of the blue, his oldest child, just out of school, announced that she was marrying the slight, silent Carey. At twenty-four, he was seven years her senior, and besides, he was a quarter-caste, dammit! And, anyway, just what did he do for a living? The Dooligan farm was only a tangle of brush and rocks where not even a rabbit would want to live.

Edith Menzies married Carey Dooligan for love; in the early days, he had a lot of that. He was a hard worker, too, being acutely aware of the district's feeling against him and his white wife. Deep down he was also ashamed of his heritage, so he worked and sweated until he had cleared roughly a quarter of his land.

Those were happy times, with the young girl wife bringing out lunch on horseback for her slender dark man. He would smile and his eyes would dance with his dreams and he would whistle like the birds in the bush.

At night she would teach him what she had learned at school, because he had rarely attended the shanty school in town. Old Tom would mumble stories about the old days and old Mary would sit like a shadow, just as she always did.

Carey went to his first auction and bought twenty cows and a decrepit old bull. But the ancient one did his job, and by next spring the herd had increased by ten. Carey bought some sheep and a few pigs, put a crop in and cleared more land. But all the schemes were his wife's for she had more business sense than he.

Interspersed with all the work was leisure: dances and gymkhanas, picnics, cricket and football matches, movies, the race meet at Yarramingup every year.

Gradually the people of the district accepted the marriage. It was difficult not to like Carey, with his lanky form and friendly smile. Besides, the district respected the Menzies family and nobody wanted to hurt Carey's wife and, as time passed, his three children.

Carey kept away from his Aboriginal relatives and they kept away from him. Occasionally one of them would turn up for a yarn and a feed and a look at their nephews and niece — and, as often as not, to borrow some of Carey's hard-earned money. Deirdre and Dobie Greyboy came down sometimes, their ute loaded up with wild dark waifs. Dobie still had his hopes and dreams, but was searching desperately to realise them; Deirdre had given up.

By the time Doug was born, both his Menzies aunts were married with children, so he had a choice of playmates: either those from the reserve or those in 'the big hoose', as John Menzies' mansion was called by the Dooligans, but he usually played by himself.

Carey's house had six rooms, three of them the original slab hut built by old Tom. The Dooligans never had enough money to build a nice house, such as Edith dreamed of, for all the money went back into the farm.

Sometimes the roof leaked and the house was always cold in winter. Then, in summer, it was too dusty and snakes were everywhere. But it was home.

Edith rarely had pretty dresses. She could never invite her old friends over for a visit and she was seldom asked to small private parties. She and her husband were tolerated at dances, but they were never invited to the bridge games her sisters attended or, if they were, they were slyly stared at, which was worse than not going at all.

But she had her man; he was happy and simple and loved everyone. Not understanding the rebuffs he sometimes encountered, he would come to her and she would help with her words and touches of kindness. And she had her children and the garden that she loved as a fourth child. She nurtured her children with milk and love, and her garden with love and water, and was content.

Then Carey gave up.

First of all Tommy died, which had shattered him. He was getting old, and he had hoped that Tommy would help him on the farm when he came home, for skinny little Doug was no good, off living in a fantasy world by the river or pond or in the bush all day. Then there had been the drought. Most of the bigger farms had got over it, but Carey had had to borrow from the bank. It had been a difficult struggle, the price being either the death of his pride or the death of his land.

Carey would go for long walks or rides into the majestic countryside, alone and frail. He hardly talked to his wife or children any more. Often he went to the town hotel to drink by himself, so when he was at home he was always drunk.

Doug would drive the ute around the small property, checking stock and fences, while his Dad was off on a wander or a binge. The boy grew to love his land as much as his father once had.

That is why it hurt him more than anyone else when his father announced, one morning, that he was selling the farm and they were moving up to Perth.

Doug was only twelve then, and it hurt to be torn from the earth he cherished. In their new house, in East Perth, he missed the swaying trees and the choirs of birds. The sheep bleating and cattle lowing, whistling across the clear, tangy morning air. Most of all he missed the cool brown pool where, it was said, the ancient tribes had come for initiation ceremonies.

His Dad wandered away more often and for longer, until he never came home at all. He stayed out at Deirdre's most of the time. Now he drinks metho.

Doug often likes to remember his father as he was: shooting kangaroos, then skinning them by the red light of a seductive fire; at football matches, Doug perched like Long John Silver's parrot on a bony shoulder, with his father cackling and grinning like a pirate and jumping about in ecstasy. Doug and his father alone together, bringing in the sheep or cattle or putting up a fence. No words, just thoughts — and thoughts are often like clouds, bringing hopes of rain, then evaporating until there is nothing but hard, blue emptiness.

Not much to go on really, Doug's memories of his father.

The last memory is of a broken, shabby old man, crouched against the shady wall away across the yard full of green-clad, dead-eyed men. That is the memory he wants most to forget, but it is the truest.

What a waste of a life, thinks Doug. What happened to all his father's visions of owning his special little piece of country that had all belonged to his ancestors once, anyhow? Of walking down the gusty streets of the town, as proud as any king?

Gone. All gone. Shattered and winking as wickedly as a broken metho bottle from the darkest, dirtiest gutter.

Edith looks across at her last son and thinks how like Carey he is, in the threadbare clothes; with his lean, empty face. In his eyes there is a glimmering, like movement far back in a cave. So one cannot see anything yet knows that what is there is dangerous. Yes, he has changed, she thinks.

'So what are you going to do now, Doug? I suppose you should find a job?'

'Yeah, they put me on the dole, when I come out. I'll just wander around,' he tells her.

'Well, you're nineteen now, Douglas. You should think about a permanent job. You can't live on the dole all your life.'

He smiles at his own dream.

'Wouldn't mind buyin' a piece of land one day. All of me own. Like before,' he says softly.

'What rot,' she cries, for that life is behind her now. 'How on earth can you expect to buy some land when you haven't a brass penny to your name?'

'I have, too,' he retorts, upset because she has destroyed one of the things that held him together inside.

'I got prison pay,' he blurts out, then wishes he hadn't, because all his prison pay as well as the fifty dollar dole cheque he has received is rolling fetidly around in his belly or in the bellies of his friends or all his cousins.

'Well? Where is it, then?' she asks, politely. 'It would be nice if you could buy some food.'

'Yeah. Well, um, it's all gone, see.'

'Oh?'

There is an uncomfortable pause.

'Well, I 'ad to see my friends, didn't I?' he sulks defensively. He has to close the door so no-one can get inside his mind.

'I see,' she says.

'Anyways, I been locked up for two years, nearly, and I wanted a bit of fun. It's my life, ain't it? Why doesn't everyone leave me alone?'

'You're not drunk now, Douglas, so you can't have been drinking and having fun today,' her gentle voice reasons, and her peaceful eyes engulf him like enchanted lakes. But it is too late. He has retreated into himself like a tortoise. There is just a hard shell of resentment; the music of her wisdom beats vainly on his soul.

'I'm not angry with you, Doug. Just surprised that you should find it in your heart to lie to me, your mother,' her soft voice drones on. 'You see, I knew you came out yesterday, because your parole officer rang up to remind you to report on Friday. I think he'd take a very dim view of your association with Sylvester Jackson and Floyd Davey and all the Greyboys, Tarriots and Camptons.'

'Yeah, well, it's none of 'is bloody business. The Greyboys and Tarriots just 'appen to be my cousins, as well as your nephews and nieces. Ya forgot about our black 'lations, Mum, ya so 'igh and mighty now?'

His words flow out angrily. She always makes him angry and this puzzles him for he does love her. She is all he has left from his long-ago Utopia.

'No, I haven't forgotten. It seems to me *you* have forgotten a few things, though. Forgotten that Hughie Tarriot is a known criminal, with a record of dangerous assaults; that Lennard and Jason and Tiny are all treading a thin line, and are sure candidates for jail; that you have been released earlier than expected on the understanding that you keep away from your old haunts. But it seems you haven't forgotten your childish tantrums and your cruel words that have hurt your family so often. I thought you were a man now, but I'm mistaken.'

He *is* a man. A bumbling, unsure man, it is true, but a man all the same.

He can drink at hotels and vote and go to R certificate films or betting shops. He can get his driver's licence and get married and sign documents. If he doesn't look out he will 'defend his beaches with his last round', if he gets called up when the next war starts.

He turned eighteen when he was in solitary for smashing up the cell he was in, after it all got too much for him once. All the presents he had were a Bible and a shit bucket and a cold, hard bed.

Happy birthday, Doug.

But that is one thing he will never tell anyone. Only he and the ghosts of his grandfather and his brother know about that nightmare, because he thought of them all the fourteen days and nights that he was confined in the separate, cruel, yard and the tiny cell. He relived his memories of a loud, red man, with faded blue cheerful eyes and with some auburn in his white hair still; sitting on a knee and listening to stories told in the lilting Irish voice, on the small, sunny verandah; and the songs his grandfather would croak out about love and bold Fenian men. Then another Tom, skinnier and darker, with kind brown eyes; playing football or chasey or hide-and-seek; sneaking a few puffs of forbidden cigarettes, in the dusty, sweet-smelling darkness of the hayshed, their own private hideaway that only the rats and the mice knew about. Tommy had looked after him almost from the day he was born.

Doug gets up and goes to his mother, who is so feeble and so pale and so alone. Where is her husband? Where are her children? Where, oh where, is her garden? Only her ornaments, adorning the shelves, and photos and the paintings on the wall, are truly hers. They cluster silently like crows on a fence, waiting for her to die.

He puts a claw-like hand upon her shoulder but she is remote in her unhappiness.

'Look, I'm sorry, Mum. I should of come 'ome, yeah, but I was thinkin', see?'

'You hurt me, Douglas. I am *not* high and mighty at all,' she whispers. 'When you were in jail, the Greyboys used to come around here all the time with their problems, and I would help them as best I could. Deirdre came around once or twice to see me and tell me about Carey. I got Tiny out of trouble God knows how many times and paid all of Lennard's fines and bailed Jason out, whenever he went in for street drinking, and looked after Hughie's girl, when he went to Bunbury regional prison late last year, and . . . Oh! it just goes on and on and never stops! How do you think my friends feel when a sniffling little half-caste girl creeps in here asking for money or help for her man? When the police are coming around here every second day? Do you think I like this kind of life?' she cries.

'It's all over now, Mum, it's all over now. Ya don't 'ave to worry any more,' he mumbles ineffectively.

'Is it?' Wet eyes look at and through him. 'It's already started, and you haven't even been twenty-four hours out of jail.'

'Oh, well,' is all he can say. All he can do is turn his back on her and pick up the battered, broken brown case that holds all his worldly possessions.

'I'm goin' to 'ave a sleep in my room, anyways.'

He is gone, and she is truly alone again. He tried to reach you, she thinks, in his own cautious way, and you lost him. She drinks her cold coffee and tries not to cry.

Doug's room is out on the verandah. It has walls of thin asbestos and is only a makeshift place, but it is his own. During his absence, it has been used as a store room and various boxes huddle against the walls. But his posters of Elvis and Abba still cling to the brick wall of the house like spiders, just as the room clings to the house itself. The room and the boy are the same: cold and unwanted.

He flings himself disconsolately onto the squeaking bed that takes up almost the entire room. The mattress is lumpy and there is a depressing air about the place.

All his own. He has no one to share things with. He grins at the mass of dusty cobwebs in the corner of the roof and breathes in the dust of the months of disuse and emptiness. Here, on this very bed, he lost his virginity to Jenny Campton: musky, salacious Jenny Campton, with the huge, soft breasts and dark twisting legs and her mouth that was like the river of Lethe, tasting and forgetting as they rolled amongst the dirty, tangled blankets.

Sometimes this room has been crowded with as many as seven people, black and brown bodies all over the bed and floor (sometimes in the strangest of positions) after a late night in town.

But tonight there is only Doug Dooligan. His days are almost over now. All his friends are married or pregnant, and there is a new generation of youthful revellers dancing and dodging down the streets. It seems that even Floyd Davey, the Pretty Boy himself, is settling down with a woman.

Those days were fun. Seductive giggles and silent shadows; the clink of dreams — red, white or gold. His music was the whizz and zip of pinball machines or the loud throbbing of discos, where he rolled like a silver ball amidst the flashing ultra-violet lights. If he got a good score he ended up warm with a woman in bed, and, if he lost, there were other endless nights, for he was seventeen and as free as an eagle circling broken clouds.

Then he had the fight.

It was show time: the Perth Royal Show, with its showbags and bands and fireworks and the animal displays that were the core of the whole week's activities. People came from everywhere. The noise and excitement of sideshow alley attracted all the young, shiftless street people who were always on the lookout for a bit of fun.

Pretty Boy's gang slithered down the grassy embankment of the railway line and climbed over where the tin fence around the grounds bent like a crooked finger, beckoning them to sample all kinds of sweets. They were rich enough, as Floyd, Doug and Silver had gone on a breaking and entering spree the day before, netting about three hundred dollars among them.

The lights and noise of the sideshows drew them like flowers attract butterflies and, like butterflies, it seemed that they could not stay still or else they would die. This was the first time Doug had a girlfriend to share his day, so he was doubly happy. They went in the Ghost Train, where Doug hit the gorilla with an empty Coke can. They went on the Ferris wheel, where they shared one of Silver's joints, and felt like gods, up in the black sky, with lights and Perth grovelling all around them.

Floyd rocked the basket so much when they were at their highest point that Doug thought they would fall out. Jenny Campton screamed and screamed while Pretty Boy and Silver laughed at their fear.

They really enjoyed themselves, going on every ride there was, it seemed — especially the go-karts. They tried their luck at the stalls: shooting guns, spearing cards, knocking down tins or coconuts. Only Doug fluked a win, a hideous pink bear for his lady love.

Just outside the boxing tent, Doug stopped to gaze at and dream about all the painted heroes upon the forlornly flapping canvas. The tent was closed until the next day, and the flattened area around was bare except for empty cans and screwed-up paper.

Doug was thinking about how he would look in shorts and gloves, glowering on the canvas. Jenny stood beside him, knowing his moods and happy to wait while she rolled a smoke. Floyd and Silver grinned at each other and slid away; perhaps Doug might want to take advantage of one of the many dark spots around for a quick kiss and cuddle.

Someone cannoned into Jenny and sent her sprawling, her cigarette sailing through the air and her new pink bear falling into a lonely puddle of morning rain. It embraced the furry creature with clammy, muddy hands.

There was no-one to embrace Jenny, though. Doug, dragged

from his reverie, spun around to take in the scene.

'Oo the fuck are you pushing, you black moll?' a voice rasped like a rusty old saw.

Doug's eyes, still bright from his dreams, focused on the gang of leering skinheads who had nonchalantly formed a semi-circle around the two.

They had come from Fremantle that morning, stomping and romping like wild horses, out to find a fight they could win or a woman they could root. Now it seemed they had found both at the same time.

Skinny Doug hunched into his clothes and stared bleakly at the grinning, shaven-headed, big-booted white boys. A few passers-by stopped to watch curiously, but most of them scurried away from the danger zone. The music from the show leaped and shimmered like imps, slid like snakes and sprang like gremlins around the silent tableau.

'Oh, look, Joey, she dropped her Teddy bear,' one of the boys said, mock-reproachful. 'You shouldn't ought to of done that,' and he bent and picked up the sodden prize that had been won with such joy and laughter. With a grin like a starving wolf, he handed it to Jenny, who took it silently, with large, fearful eyes and backed towards Doug.

'Don't yer fink Benny deserves a kiss fer savin' yer bear from drownin', Mary?' another retorted, amidst chuckles.

'Her true love might not like that,' said a third.

'You her boyfriend, you skinny little gin-jockey shit?' sneered Joey as the gang moved closer.

Doug's hand fell lovingly over his grandfather's cut-throat razor snuggling in his pocket. All the members of Floyd's gang carried a weapon. It made them feel really big to be risking a sentence if the cops caught them armed with dangerous weapons in public. Pretty Boy Floyd had a pocket knife honed as sharp as his cunning, and Silver had a flick-knife he had bought from Taiwan Hui. But Doug had his grandfather's old-fashioned razor, a lethal weapon indeed.

'Fuck off,' he muttered. The skinheads laughed. They

intended to beat up this weedy pale youth and root his fat black boong senseless; that should be a pretty good night.

Joey closed in. In a blur of white his face was slashed open while Jenny screamed and Doug's shiny razor dripped red.

The other youths were stunned at this show of violence and, as they stood there, Doug struck again. This time Benny went down, yelling, with a cut across his stomach. Then the other eight boys came in like dogs around a kangaroo.

Jenny went screaming off, crying for Floyd and Silver.

Doug went under.

It was a brutal fight. Doug's razor found one more victim before beefy hands tore it from his grasp and a blow from a piece of iron stupefied him. He was helpless for a few vital seconds while blows and kicks rained upon his puny body.

Then big Floyd leapt like the devil into the pack, crashing two heads together and sending their owners reeling. Stocky Silver took on one more and two of the Greyboys took on the rest.

Into Doug's blurred, frightened vision swam an ugly, angry red face. Joining his knobbly fists together, he connected with the face and the skinhead went crashing back into the silent fighters dashed on the canvas tent.

Doug had never been more afraid in his life. For all he knew, his quick hands might have killed someone. He had only meant to flash the razor close to the face of his enemy, frightening him.

Too late now.

In his fear, he forgot everything: the show, the lights, the people and Jenny Campton, big-eyed in the background. He saw only the fat squirming boy on the ground before him, howling hideously.

His boots beat out a tattoo of victory upon the pale body. At every thud and gasp he became more of a man. He would kill this person who had dared to laugh at him and his girl; tonight, while the solemn moon awful in its silence stared down. Then he would be remembered for evermore.

But instead he was treated with hate and contempt and fear by the police who dragged him from the bruised, unconscious boy, and by the magistrate, in court the following week, when all his rage had died away.

No Thor or Mars or God of War was he.

Just a lanky, sorrowful child of the streets, blown like chaff by any wind.

Joey lost his eye and would have a mean scar to the end of his days. Benny was in great pain in Royal Perth Hospital, and the other boy was still only semi-conscious and had several broken bones.

Doug was detained until the Governor's pleasure.

He appealed, lost and was forgotten.

But now Doug Dooligan is outside and free again.

The rain starts to fall heavily. When it rained at night on the roof of the cells, he never felt more lonely, but the rain today is friendly, since he lies on his own bed in his own room while the darkness closes around him like a lover.

He listens to the radio that he bought just last week inside the prison. He listens to the music of the rain.

His eyes turn inwards like Riley Keeley's rejected brother. The music blankets him.

Clickety-clickety-clack. High-heeled shoes patter upon the verandah slabs and the door opens.

'I brought you some blankets, Doug. It gets quite cold here at night sometimes.'

His mother is too quick and she sees his eyes peeled back so all their truthfulness shows in their agony. He cannot look at her.

'Thanks, Mum.'

'You've a new radio.'

'Yeah,' a sly smile drifts over his face. 'First thing I never stole for ages. I bought it off Danny Forsyth for fifty packets of smokes. It's got a tape recorder too, see' he says proudly and she senses that they are friends again.

4

For a week Doug hangs around the house, watching TV mostly, reading endless comics and listening to endless music on the radio that squats like a black god above his dirty bed.

On Friday he goes to see Mr Salvadorez, his parole officer.

The Probation and Parole office is way up the other end of town, in the dead part of Perth. There are no nightclubs or cinemas or discos here; just square, cold buildings on empty grey streets.

He shuffles up in the rain and wishes he was back in jail, where at least he would be able to shelter. But not really. Bugger jail. He thinks he might go and see Pretty Boy and Silver after his session.

He wonders what his parole officer will be like. He will probably be all suit and tie and shiny shoes, with words as empty as his life. Doug might as well be a rotten apple lying on the ground, he thinks, for all his parole officer will care.

Sniff gloomily and squat under the bridge that throws a heavy arm languidly across the road. Roll a smoke and watch two pretty girls clatter by.

He thinks of Polly's young firm body and big eyes. As soon as his cheque comes, next week, he will go and see her again. Doug wonders whether Silver will be going with her by then. He hopes not.

Time to move on again.

Skinny little box trees crouch by the kerb and shake their pitiful heads like their bigger brethren. No-one takes any notice of them.

A cool drink can crashes loudly down the hill, hand in hand with the wind. It gets a quick look from passers-by, then dismissal. It bounces against the kerb and is as still as death.

That's what life is like; empty hollow noises where you thought there was joy and something special, then just nothing. And no-one gives a shit, not really.

He shuffles through the glass door and goes up the stairs.

A young, friendly woman sits at the desk; she charms Doug with a smile, takes his name and asks him to wait.

The waiting-room is small. A table of magazines, like an altar full of offerings, stands in the middle. Older, hardened crims and younger men than Doug (probably only on probation) trying to match their elders in fierceness, lounge around the wall. One bewildered boy is wondering what he is doing there. No nyoon-gahs, though.

Doug slumps in a corner and rolls another smoke. Someone cadges a cigarette from him. Just like being back in bloody jail, he thinks, but hands over his depleted packet. We're all the same, after all; murderers, thieves, rapists, mother fuckers, father-fuckers and sons of bitches, every last one.

At last a short, pudgy man, with worried, weary eyes hiding behind glasses, steps in and calls him out.

Eyes follow him as he leaves.

In a little cubicle of a room, he is offered a seat and a watery smile.

'Sit down, uh, Doug. This is just a get-to-know-you meeting and it won't take long. Now, my name's Emmanuello Salvadorez, but if that's too big a mouthful then just call me Manuel.'

The man looks the silent, sullen boy over.

Got a right one here, he thinks. Sentenced indefinitely and did two years, almost. Doesn't look the type to half kill someone, but you never can tell. Look at that Macedonian boy I had before; quiet as a lamb and it turned out he strangled his girlfriend with her own stocking.

Doug's eyes flick at the man, then he stares at the iron filing cabinet. Let him get his look over, and then I can go home, he thinks.

'You were in for fighting, I believe, Doug. You shouldn't fight because it doesn't get you anywhere.'

'They was pickin' my woman,' he grunts.

'Yes.'

There is nothing else to say.

'Did you ever go to school, Doug?'

'Nuh. When Dad come up 'ere I never went to school much, anyways. School don't teach ya fuck all. Jail is where I learned all my lessons.' Doug smiles cheekily.

Try again.

'Your father's part-Aboriginal, I believe?' says Mr Salvadorez.

'Yeah. Never seen *him* for ages. Not for five years nearly. Seen 'im one time in Freo, but he was too far away. I never liked 'im, anyways. Tell ya funny thing; my Dad used to jar me up and nag, nag, nag, for 'angin' around with Silver Jackson because Silver's Dad was a wife basher and murderer and 'is Mum was just an old alcoholic, ya know. Anyways, 'e can talk now, or what?' Doug chuckles softly. 'Biggest alky in Guildford, my Dad is.'

'Well, that's it, Doug. You know, you seem to have a fine mother. Do you want to turn out like your father? You should really have another go at finishing school. You could get a job during the day and go to classes at night.' Mr Salvadorez says earnestly.

'Could,' Doug says hesitantly to the cabinet. The truth is that he just wants to have fun for a while. Play pinball and pool, get drunk, be with his girlfriend. Forget about life for a while, and frolic like a child in a field of daisies; with the city lights fluttering like flowers all around him and buildings nodding sleepily. He wants to be king of his own domain, with his own joys, for a brief time.

'Now listen, Doug,' Mr Salvadorez says, and does not continue until the youth's mistrustful eyes are upon him. 'You've been given a chance to straighten out your life, and it's my job to see you do. I mean, goodness, you're only just nineteen and what have you done with yourself in your most exciting years? Eighteen months' jail. Now I understand that it can be extremely traumatic stepping out into a busy life after that, but I want you to understand that it is not too late to start again.' He pauses.

Not a word has sunk in. Doug sits there, with vacant grey eyes and smoke dribbling from his thin mouth.

'You're advised not to see Davey or Jackson either', says Mr Salvadorez. 'Nor is it the best idea to see your cousins at Guildford.'

Doug is about to say something but he bites it back. This man wouldn't understand, anyway. He wouldn't see that friends are even more important than money in Doug's world. With friends around you, you can be king or jester and it's all the same. Mates, girls, cars and drink: that is all you need to make life go around.

So Doug sniffs and shrugs his shoulders, which Mr Salvadorez takes as agreement. He smiles brightly.

'I understand, also, you worked in the prison garden and are quite an avid gardener. Quite a green fingers, I should say.'

Doug gives him a real smile, looking him in the eyes for the first time.

'Yeah. Well, ya see, it makes ya feel good when one seed comes up, all green and pretty and grows into a flower or fruit or something. Ya know, ya made that thing, see? It's like ya woman 'avin' ya baby.'

'Have you got a girlfriend, Doug?'

'Aaaah, dunno,' he mutters, sliding back into himself.

'You said you went to jail for defending your girlfriend.'

'Yeah,' he murmurs. 'Before, I 'ad one solid girl, but she changed now.' He thinks of the old Jenny and the fun they used to have. 'Naw, things change. Everything changes.'

'Well, let's hope you change for the better.' Mr Salvadorez smiles and stands, as does Doug. 'Remember, Doug, I'm here to help you. If you get into trouble you must ring me at once. Now, you can't leave the State at all on parole, and you must contact me before you go on any long journeys within the state. Meanwhile, I'll look out for a job — perhaps gardening or working in a nursery.'

He is rewarded with a grin and happy eyes shine at him.

'Righty-oh. See ya, then'.

'Every Friday, Doug.'

'Yeah.'

Then like a shadow, the thin youth is gone.

He's out in the street again. Leaves whirl past him on the run. Everything's on the run, from the billowing grey clouds that make the afternoon dark to the crumpled pieces of paper that kept chips or pies warm.

He wouldn't mind a feed now. Not much money left, though.

Just as he reaches the sooty fringe of Perth proper, he comes across a brightly-painted food shop and ambles in.

The owner eyes him suspiciously, but Doug, thinking about his might-be job as a gardener, does not notice. He finds his last few cents and gets his pie. Ignoring his held-out hand, the shopkeeper spills his change all over the counter. Doug's eyes go cold and blank as the insult sinks home.

'Somphin' else you wan'?'

The youth chews on his bottom lip.

'Huh?' insists the shopkeeper.

'This pie is cold as ice, mate.'

'Machine, itsa broke.'

Doug's fingers scoop up the change and he eyes the mocking, olive man over carefully. One night, when he is drunk, he will kick his head in if he sees him.

The shopkeeper must be Italian or Macedonian. Neither race likes the Aboriginals, although the Italian fettlers down south haven't seemed to mind the women so much.

Back in town Doug decides to wait and see if Pretty Boy and Silver and the girls come in.

He hangs around one of the pinball parlours, owned by Gary, a friendly man who makes everyone welcome. It is only a small place, lit with green lights. It is downstairs, with its door gaping onto the street like a hungry mouth, eating up all the lonely people.

About four o'clock his cousins thump and bang down the stairs like a herd of kangaroos. They have the same quiet pride you see in kangaroos' eyes and, when they want to, they can glide into the alleyways and lose themselves as easily as a kangaroo in the bush.

'Well, bugger me dead!' cries Lennard. 'Ya still livin', Dougie? The way Willice and Jerry was talkin' I'd of thought ya was dead.'

'Ya should of 'eard Jenny Campton when ya left', joins in Jason. 'She were gunna kill 'erself with a bottle, unna.'

'Too mad, boy. 'Where's my man? Where my man? I mardong for my man, Doug Dooooligan,' Tiny shrieks like an old crone.

'Tchooo-choo, Tiny. Keep it down,' Doug hisses, embarrassed, but he might as well be talking to the pinball machine.

All the Greyboys like to let the world know that they are around, unless they are stealing. Otherwise the world and life would pass them by as though they were dull stones by the river's edge. But the Greyboys and Tarriots croak like frogs and wait eternally for tomorrow's princess.

The Greyboys have the same thin build as all the Dooligan clan and their hair colour varies between their mother's red, their father's blond, or their ancestors' raven black. No-one knows why the Tarriots are the Dooligans' cousins; something about their being Dobie Greyboy's cousins, really. And, then, Frankie Dooligan, the oldest brother, was living with Margaret Tarriot and she gave him four children before he wandered away. Still, Hughie Tarriot is a good bloke to have beside you in a fight and Glenn always has lots of money and a nice big car. Besides, everyone turns out to be a cousin, sooner or later.

'Ya seen Pretty Boy yet?' Lennard asks. ''E's grown cruel big, unna? When me and 'im was in Riverbank one time, I was bigger than 'im. But now — fuck 'im!'

'I reckon 'e'd give even 'Ughie a fair rip, unna?' Tiny says.

'Yeah,' mutters Doug.

It is important, the welfare of their bodies. They admire strength and skill and are always commenting on how good a fighter this man or that man is. They are always fighting in the back streets and alleys and parks.

'You grown too, ya bastard!' Jason thumps him and Doug smells the stale beer and fresh wine on the youngster's breath. Never one to let a chance go by, he smiles and says.

'Yeah, J-man, what about a charge for ya favourite cousin?'

'Later on, buddy. I'm goin' to grab a moony tonight.' The child gives Doug what he thinks is a manly nudge, but nearly falls over as he does.

'Only thing you'll grab is ya doodle,' grins Tiny.

'Well, at least I got a doodle to grab, ya poofter.'

Smiles dash whitely across the brown faces and the two brothers pretend to wrestle for a moment. Micky, the quietest of the brothers, as well as the oldest at twenty-one, puts on the theme song from *Prisoner* and stands by the jukebox. He silently thinks of his woman, who got six months in Niandi for assault.

Lennard purses his lips at Micky's back when the song starts playing. The brothers grin but no-one is willing to tease the dour Micky openly.

More people troop downstairs. This is the nyoongah hangout now. It used to be the Crystal Palace, just up the road and around the corner, but that has become a trendys' place, with a disco and electronic spacial games. So like black mist in the morning, the children of the shadows have faded away from there. They much prefer the green moon of Gary's place and Gary's jokes and smiles.

Like a magician, Gary sits behind his desk. From his bag come silver spells to turn the holder into a pirate or a racing car driver or a cowboy or the bionic man. Or a girl's dream will come true, floating through the air in a parade of guitar and drum music while the jukebox chews up another twenty cent piece. Down here people can be whatever they want.

Doug forgets about his mother and her anxious eyes.

When it gets dark and the cousins have used up nearly all their meagre money, when Micky has listened to his fill of songs about love and faraway eyes and honey lips, they all troop out onto the crowded street.

It's Friday night, the big night in the city, when all the tribesmen meet.

A big mob of girls and boys cuddle together around the doorway and keep an eye open for police, pretty cars or even prettier girls.

The cousins treat their kingdom like the hunters they are.

'Come on, J-man, what about this charge?' cries Tiny, so young Jason shoulders the glass door aside and swaggers into the bottle shop like Butch Cassidy or the Sundance Kid.

Armed with a flagon, they creep up an unwanted alley and sip at a little joy. They joke and laugh and talk about what is going on at Lockridge camp.

This is a new generation now of loud, brash children. Two years ago, when Silver and Pretty Boy and Doug were in their warlike prime, these youths used to play quiet pool or run about the streets playing kids' games and thinking about hot, new love.

Now the love is cold and they are men. No-one owns them. They are their own bosses. They have cobwebs in their hair and minds and, spiderlike, they dream up new dastardly deeds for their initiation. They paint on lies and blood from fights, to make themselves look elegant with patterns from their new Dreaming. They dance to their gods of flashing lights and hopes. The city, squatting like elders around a campfire, has cut off their childhood: it imparted the legends from the alleys and the parks and the third-rate slum houses and the police stations and the jails, as the elders of the past imparted the legends of the land and the law to the ancestors of these youths. So they are truly men in their new country.

A single light blinks off the upturned V.O. Port flagon. A ruby that no-one can ever own but only look at is formed; a ruby eye glaring at the world. The boys worship their one-eyed god, then sacrifice the dry, white husk of all their delusions so it shatters against the black end of the alley.

44

They walk around the streets, going nowhere. Meet a few acquaintances here and there, burn a few cigarettes and hear a few more yarns.

'The Keeleys and Dawsons had a big fight down at Pinjarra last weekend, and busted half the town up' . . . 'Jimmy Orrellie was up for stealing more than two hundred cars. Monaych come for him, with guns and all, and Jimmy's brother, Shaun, pulled a big machete on one cop so he went in for assault' . . .

'Susan Smith was raped by two wadgula boys out at Scarborough beach. All her brothers come in looking for this white panel van and wouldn't they make those white boys piss . . . Little Dicky Campton raped a thirty-six-year-old woman and now he's crying every night in Riverbank . . . Now you boys have never seen a prettier little thing than that, wriggling down the road, unna?' . . . Whew, buddah . . . What you reckon about Rhodesia becoming their own country? after seven years' battle, mind you? . . . Who's Rhodesia? . . . No, true, 'I reckon it would be good to be a guerrilla and go to war . . . Me, I'd get a machine gun and shoot the Boys from Brazil: phut, phut. Right in the fuckin' head, too . . .

'You hear what happened to Johnny Rhyne? He opened the door and all those Nyler boys was there and they shot him dead in the guts. Poor bastard. Big kill now. Well, Johnny got no people . . . Hey, look at that solid machine . . .'

Just talk, like leaves blowing in the wind.

Pretty Boy Floyd comes into town with his fiery eyes and proud strut and sly smile. He latches onto his mate, the stumbling Doug.

'Where ya bin all week, budda? Polly gettin' 'ot for ya, meantime,' he smiles, while the Greyboys laugh.

'Look out for Doug! One week out of jail and ya got womans all over Perth fightin' for ya,' Tiny yelps.

'Might be cos 'e's the Incredible Hulk, or what.' Jason guffaws and starts choking so that Micky has to thump his back.

'She's lyin' there all alone,' Floyd whispers. 'Yorrn, she most probably thinkin' 'er bad mean man gone back to jail.'

'Back to ya boyfriend, unna, Doug?' someone cries.

'Yeah, Philip Berry,' chuckles another.

'True, eh? Sell ya me bum for a packet of Drum,' Lennard chants.

'I wouldn't fuck you if ya give me two.' Another flash of nasal wit comes from the back of the crowd, so the group falls about laughing.

So noisy are they that the Boys from Brazil pull over to the kerb, suspicious.

The Boys from Brazil are CIB men; not the original Boys, who numbered five and were split up after their activities were given too much publicity. These three are bad enough, though. Once they make an enemy or mark someone, they never let up. They are rough, too, and proud of their roughness. They despise the coloured youths with whom they come in contact and the Aboriginal youths fear these three as much as they would have feared the woodarchi of their ancestors that hid in the rocks and were evil.

They gather around the now sullen, silent crowd of youths, some of whom still laugh softly at the joke, some of whom puff nervously on cigarettes or fidget. All of them are more or less nervous because all have heard of, if not tasted, the law of the Boys from Brazil.

Their routine is the same as ever. There's a big heavy, who is usually the driver because he cannot run fast, and two smaller men, one of whom is the supposedly good guy. He never slaps the victim around, but talks gently to him.

'What's goin' on here? A fucking corroboree?' the big driver sneers.

'Do any of you buggers know a Colin Moriarty?' the small, evil man growls, glaring around the group.

'No,' sniffs Colin, wondering who has dobbed him in.

'Well, you boys had better get on home,' the quiet man advises.

'Yeah, make a move. Piss off,' chips in the driver.

Doug hugs his old coat around him. His eyes are angry. He

hawks and spits and mutters:

'Why? We not doin' no 'arm. It's a free world, mate. Me and my cousins can stand where we like.'

The three detectives descend on him so that he is back to back with the wall of a small alcove. The other youths drift away except for Micky Greyboy and Floyd. They wait in a doorway just far enough away not to be dragged in too.

'Oo the fuck are you, smart-arse?' the smaller man grates.

'Douglas Dooligan,' he murmers in pride, for he has a 'name' now, and a record, and the right to speak out.

'I know you. You just came out of jail, didn't you, Douglas?' The quiet man scrutinises him with deep blue eyes.

Doug nods and drags on a cigarette that is suddenly knocked from his grasp.

'You should have better manners, then, and call us 'sir'. Which dunny did you crawl from anyway?' snarls the driver. 'You've been drinking too?'

'Nuh.'

'Don't lie! What do you think we are, stupid or something? We should take you down to Central for street drinking and teach you some manners.'

'I'll tell you what, Doug,' murmurs the quiet man again, 'I'm going to keep my eye on you.'

'What?' Doug mutters back, still defiant, 'you think I'm goin' on to bigger and better things?' A forced smile lifts his lips a little just to show he is not afraid of these loud-mouthed, heavy-booted keepers of the law.

'Who knows?' the man smiles back, while his eyes search the boy's face.

'You just piss off home now, sonny, or we'll run you in,' the driver glowers.

'What for?'

'Oh, never you mind, Doug, me old son. We'll think of something,' winks the small, evil one. 'Put you back in Freo, where mad bastards like you belong.'

Doug feels cold in the stomach. That is his one weak point: he

47

has vowed he will never go back to jail. He stands there while the Boys from Brazil saunter back to their car and glide away. Then Pretty Boy and Micky join him.

'What did they say, cousin? Ya want to look out for those wackers. They hate us nigs, if that ain't the truth, especially any Greyboy people, after what Franklin and Hughie Tarriot did to them,' Micky says.

'Ya fuck everything up, Dougie,' Floyd complains. 'If ya'd shut ya mouth, we'd of been right. Now those bastards will be following us all night.'

'Well it's a free world, ain't it?' Doug flares again, getting angry. 'No-one's pushin' me around ever again, Floyd. No monaych, no demons, or *no-o-o-body*.'

'Ahh, shit, ya such a big shot, unna?' hisses Floyd. His knobbly hands grab a fistful of dirty shirt and he drags Doug up off his feet, so he is standing on tip-toe. He breathes softly into his startled face. 'Well, I'm ya brother, ya might say, Doug, and I aren't seein' ya go back to poxy jail, see? *I* got respect, brother, but you! Ya supposed to be brainy and all, but ya walk around like a *hippy*! And ya got no sense to keep ya mouth shut, unna.'

He quietens down, and lets Doug sag against the door. 'Ya could of got us searched an' they would 'ave found this, then, look.'

He pulls out a computerised masterpiece of a watch, two necklaces and a big pile of notes. A cunning smile gleams on his dark face, reflected on the faces of Doug and Micky. In the dark place of the city, the three grins form a secret bond.

'I'll give this watch to you, buddy, and ya can give this necklace thing 'ere to ya Mum.' Pretty Boy smiles and Micky gives a discreet cough. Floyd turns happy eyes on Micky, too, and tells him, 'Cos ya woman in prison, ole buddy, I'll give ya some boya, so's ya can get blue drunk and forget.'

They depart.

Down beside the railway line near to the old signal boxes, Pretty Boy, Doug and Micky drink three bottles of green ginger wine while the scarred old peppermint tree droops over the falling-down fence like a drunkard and listens to their talk.

Afterwards, half stung up, they decide to catch a taxi and go to Floyd's woman's flat. They buy two flagons of V.O. Port and off they go.

Floyd really wants Doug's company. The tall, dignified youth, as proud and fierce as a Masai warrior, can hear in his scruffy little companion's words things he himself would like to say but cannot.

Pretty Boy muses sadly. Doug has always been a good person to know, easy on money and easy-tempered, too. Not any more. The old Doug of two years ago would not have answered those detectives back. His eyes would not have been angry, like a storm, but more dreamy — as still and peaceful as a lost lagoon. Still, Floyd thinks, when Doug sees Polly she will quieten him down, just as his own woman, Valerie Yarrup, has started to settle him down.

Floyd and Doug think of their women while a drunk Micky sleeps in the corner of the cab and dreams of his.

They cruise to the dark flats and pay the taxi. Micky stumbles out and is supported by the two younger Aboriginals.

Last week it was Doug, next week it might be Floyd. There is always some Aboriginal drunk on the streets or in the park.

They make it upstairs to Valerie's flat and crash inside, laughing and whooping. They dump a dazed Micky on the couch and Floyd goes to wake up Valerie for a drink. Doug follows.

When the light flicks on, he sees white Silver poised over Polly's naked body. She sees him at exactly the same moment.

He looks at Floyd, who watches him with non-committal black eyes. He goes back to the sitting-room and smiles weakly at Micky, who holds a flagon and sings to himself. Doug does not want to spoil Micky's happy drunk time.

Micky rarely drinks. In fact, he hardly does anything that sounds like fun. He works as a tiler, putting roofs on houses such as he can't even dream of owning because they are so flash. He is a good, quiet workman who has never been in trouble, except once in his youth when he got twenty-eight days for not paying a fine, but that hardly counts. All Micky wants is a quiet life and his wife.

49

Now she is in Niandi for assaulting a girl who got too close to her man.

So Micky drinks.

Doug flops down beside him and holds his head in his hands.

Tattooed Silver bursts out of the bedroom, clad in a pair of jeans.

'Well? What ya going to do about it?' he asks Doug.

Doug looks up and sees a silent Floyd and an anxious Polly framed in the doorway.

'Come on! You never come back, anyway,' Silver cries. 'I told you I'd get her, didn't I?'

Doug's eyes are hurt and confused. His stomach feels sour.

'Shows how much *you* love her, then,' jeers Silver. 'Well, I'm going back to bed.'

'Ya pickin' on me cousin, bub?' Micky chimes in before Silver can turn. He staggers to his feet. 'No, no, no, mate. Ya gotta go through me before ya muck about with Doug there.'

'Aaah, piss off. Who dragged you in, anyway? This isn't a fuckin' boarding house, ya know,' Silver pushes the drunk Micky so hard that he flies back against the wall.

Pandemonium breaks loose. Doug suddenly leaps upon Silver, who is advancing on the prostrate Micky. He is flung off and crashes into the table, whereupon his hand closes on a knife and he bounds in front of Silver. His eyes gleam as cruelly as the flashing blade, and he snarls, 'try me now, Silver, ya ugly fucker. Come on and let me rip ya guts out, ya big brave cunt.'

His whole thin body shakes with repressed violence and his eyes mesmerise Silver, who stands frozen to the spot.

There is neither sound nor movement. All the universe is still. Blue eyes and grey ones lock in a ferocious inner battle, each youth waiting for the other to move first.

Floyd seems to float over towards his friend, so silent is he.

'Give me the knife, Doug,' he says quietly. 'Bugger puttin' blood everywhere. We'll waste a day tomorrow cleanin' it all off.'

Doug lets his hand drop; Floyd grabs his wrist and takes the knife. Then Silver sends one of his famous right hooks crunching into Doug's face, so once again the scrawny youth is sent crashing into the table and falls half-stunned to the floor.

Floyd wraps an arm around Silver's throat and thumps him in the kidneys, so the white boy collapses, gasping for air. Floyd kneels beside him and asks gently, 'feelin' good, Silver? Can you hear me?'

A groan is his answer.

'I ought to kill ya, same way as Dougie would of, ya ignorant bastard. Me and Doug and Micky come for a peaceful drink and to see Doug's woman. Now, he lifts a slender finger and taps the tattooed woman over Silver's heart, 'I tell ya last week to leave Polly alone. If ya muck around one more time I'll kill you, bud. You know me, unna?'

Silver nods.

'Good.' Floyd pats his shoulder. 'Then take ya own woman and fuck off until Doug settles down. Come back turmorrer sometime.'

Silver doesn't wait around but scurries off, clothes in one hand and his girl, the sleepy, confused Rebecca, in the other.

Floyd heaves Doug up in his arms like a baby and drops him on his own double bed. He winks at Polly.

''E's all yours, now, sis. 'E got a mean temper on 'im, but, unna?' He shuts the door.

He straightens up the table and couch and lifts the sleeping Micky onto it, throwing a blanket over him, then turns to his woman.

'Just leaves you and me, baby,' he grins, and Valerie giggles. They disappear into Silver's room.

In the bedroom, Doug opens his eyes slowly and stares blankly at Polly.

'I wish I was dead,' he groans.

'I'm sorry, Dougie. Truly I am,' she whispers.

'Aaah, whaffor? I don't own ya. You ya own boss, unna? Just . . . ya know . . . sort of funny . . .' He gives a battered smile and tears fill her eyes.

'Scared shit out of me, pickin' up that knife,' he says slowly. 'I might of killed Silver.'

The girl's small hands flutter over his face and chest, like butterflies. Her lips press down on his; she murmurs endearments in his ear.

'It's finished now, Dougie. 'E never touched me, true as God. I was just sparked up, is all, ya know. I just really love ya, anyways,' she whispers.

He raises himself painfully onto his side and looks down at her.

'Do ya? Well, tell ya what, Nana. You and me'll stick like glue all the way through.'

He brushes away her blonde hair from her eyes and, with a finger, wipes away the hot tear that trickles down her cheek.

'Nana,' he breathes her secret name, known only to a few. See, I remembered. Same as in banana, unna?'

He lies down again. 'Too sick now, 'oney. But, if ya love a girl, then ya don't 'ave to make love all the time. If you do, that's not proper love, ya know. Tonight I just need a friend'.

He sighs, then the drink catches hold of his brain and he sleeps peacefully in her arms.

He wakes late in the morning, a cheerful sun sitting on his bed and Polly snoring lightly beside him. His jaw is an aching reminder of last night and he wonders what he will say to Silver.

The door opens gently and Floyd's face peers around it to grin at Doug.

'Ow's me bed, budda?'

'It's a hunky-dory,' Doug grins back.

'All the better to moony ya by,' Floyd laughs gently and tiptoes across the room. He sits in the sun beside Doug and appraises him with dark eyes.

'Silver's gone off with Rebecca. I reckon she'll give 'im what for, when she finds out what 'e was doin',' he grins.

'If 'e never hit Micky, it would of been OK. I could of talked to 'im, ya know. But 'e got me tempered up when 'e come for Micky. Poor bastard can't fight 'is way out of a paper bag. A wet paper bag, even.'

'Yeah. Micky left too. 'E got shamed, I think.' Floyd pats

Doug's shoulder and chuckles at Polly's snoring. 'Come and keep ya mate company. We still got a flagon left. Let these womans sleep. After, we'll go and find me brother and get a football and play in the park,' he says eagerly.

So the two youths sit down and watch TV, sipping from the flagon. A movie about Custer's last stand is on but, as the flagon goes down, the picture becomes disorientated, so the boys give up and decide to get a feed with some of the money Floyd stole the other night.

Just as they are about to leave, a heavy knocking shakes the front door.

'Nylers!' Floyd gasps. He springs for the little balcony outside, where he crouches, hidden. Doug is frozen to the spot until more knocking brings Floyd's woman out, bleary-eyed and tousle-headed, wrapped up in a sheet.

'Yeah, I'm comin', bugger ya,' she grumbles.

'Come 'ere, Doug! Grab me that knife off the table and get ready to jump, budda. I reckon it's them Nylers,' hisses Floyd.

It isn't, though. It's only the fat-gutted caretaker with the red face and hungry green eyes. He leers over Valerie, his eyes eating her slim, scantily clad body for emotional breakfast.

'Bit of noise last night, girlie. Mrs Schneider was complaining of thumping and yelling when it was well after one o'clock,' he says.

'Listen, mate,' Valerie grates, 'Anything goes wrong 'ere, ya come an' bother me. I'm not the only coloured peoples 'ere, ya know; there's the Reedes just down the way and Jerry Parkinson in the next block. But, nuh every time ya gotta come and wake me up and fuckin' make me look bad . . .'

'Well, there *was* some noise. Mrs Schneider . . .' the caretaker begins placatingly.

'Looks, Mrs Schneider wouldn't know if she was fartin', she so deaf and dumb,' Valerie interrupts.

She lets her sheet slip a little off her brown shoulder. 'Course, ya know,' she adds more softly, 'I could always leave, if ya reckon I'm noisy. It was just me and them two girls knocked the table over in the dark, is all. Ya seen them girls, unna, my sister and cousin, see. Well, we can go if Mrs Schneider reckons — '

'Oh no,' says the caretaker, tearing his eyes and thoughts from her shoulder. 'You can stay. Just try to keep a bit quiet, though, OK?'

'Orright. See ya,' says Valerie and she softly closes the door.

She knows that the caretaker watches her every day from the sanctuary of his little room, and sometimes she teases him by wearing tight jeans, shorts or provocative dresses. Once she would have gone with him, if only to get him drunk and roll him for his money. How could he complain, with his fat toady wife right there beside him downstairs?

He doesn't know yet about Pretty Boy Floyd Davey, who now swaggers in from the balcony and winks at his grinning girl.

'Ol' 'orny pants, ay? 'Ow'd 'e go when I let me sheet slip? 'Is eyes nearly fell out of 'is 'ead, true.'

'Ya the cunnin' one, Val. But ya better not be givin' that ole bunji man a bit on the side when the Pretty Boy's not 'ere,' Floyd tells her mock-seriously.

'Yeah? What ya think I am, anyways?' Valerie shrieks, hands on hips. 'But you boys better be careful or else we'll be out on our ear.'

'I'll knock 'im arse up if 'e tried that!' Floyd brags and he grabs his woman roughly and kisses her.

It seems that this time Floyd has found the woman he needs. She already has two children from other boys, but she isn't ugly and she doesn't nag and she's a good cook. What is more, she went all the way to third year at high school and is more learned than Floyd in most things. Sometimes he wanders off to other girls, as he has done time and time again since he was twelve, but he always comes back to Valerie Yarrup.

Once all her brothers mobbed him in the bedroom and kicked him half to death as he shouted and cried and bled. Valerie broke away from the brother who was holding her and fell on her man, sobbing hysterically and claiming that they would have to kick her too.

When Pretty Boy recovered he went hunting all five of Valerie's brothers — even twenty-five-year-old Benjo, who was a big shearer — and one by one beat them bloody to the ground; no quarter was asked or given.

Now there is an uneasy truce between the Yarrups and the Daveys. But the war with the Nylers carries on as it has done for generations.

There is a story that there were five sisters who all had a fight once, years ago. From that time on, all the sisters' children and their children's children kept the fight up. The older people in the camps or houses would keep the memories smouldering, like coals ready to stir up into heat. Then the younger kinsmen would burst forth like flames into flickering violence.

Sometimes the flames of violence would burn and consume victims. Like the time, seven years ago, when five men and a youth chased a Nyler boy all the way up St George's Terrace and clubbed him to death in the heart of the city. Now the culprits have served their time and are coming out of jail, the Nylers and all their people are coming out of the woodwork and the feud is starting all over again.

Though they have paid for their crime according to the law of the land, this is not the law of the People.

That is why, three weeks ago, Johnny Rhyne was shot at the door of his house and died in his young woman's arms, blood running like the rivers of Hades from his screaming mouth.

He was the youngest. The other five are all Floyd's cousins, which is why the Daveys have been brought into the feud. Not that Floyd really minds because he likes a good fight to liven up a boring existence.

The night after Johnny was shot, Floyd, the Stone brothers and Bevan Palmer went to one of the Nyler boys' houses, seeking revenge. Only three girls were there. They locked themselves in the bathroom, petrified with fear, while the boys smashed the house and furniture.

That was fun. Floyd felt like a warrior then, a yelping, leaping Zulu chieftain, supreme in his victory, avenging his kinsman and awaiting the return of the enemy, the menfolk of the house. Instead, a carload of police arrived, called by a terrified neighbour, and the youths fled.

But one of the besieged girls, through a hole an axe had made in the bathroom door, saw Floyd's dancing, frenzied body and recognised him as the boy she had gone with before. The word was passed, not to the police but to the People.

Now carloads of hard-faced young men from the South-west clatter around the streets. Perth boys make petrol bombs, and steal guns and wait.

The police worry.

5

The boys get drunk, call each other brother and laugh a lot. The girls play cards and go and get a feed for everybody at the local fish and chip shop. They sit beside their men, happy in their company. Tomorrow Doug might end up in jail again or the police might kick the door in and take Polly back to the home she hates, or the CIB might catch up with the buccaneering Pretty Boy and it'll be his turn in jail.

There is so little time. Soon enough they will be settled down with their pension cheques and bottles of beer and only their memories to keep them warm.

Later they walk over to Floyd's brother Charley's house near a huge green park that sprawls between two sloping hills and a majestic pine forest.

It's a gloriously lazy day, with a benign sun ruling his azure kingdom. Birds come out to sing and children come out to play. On one side of the park the locals play soccer. Brightly coloured teams flash and flitter like birds across the ground, sending the nimble ball weaving and trembling, twisting and winding along the ground or through the air.

At Charley's house, a chattering crowd has gathered and is perched along the wooden rails flanking the path and park. Young boys watch young girls cycle or walk past and think of times to come.

Charley is twenty and a shorter, plumper version of Floyd. He has shoulders like a bullock and would be a good boxer if he set his mind to it. But he's too placid and drinks far too much. He even drinks metho and Coke every once in a while.

All he cares about is his girl and little baby and whatever job he can hold for the moment. He is forever on the move, wandering off one day to a new and better town, then becoming disillusioned or homesick or just suffering from itchy feet, a phenomenon too complicated for him to explain. Every nyoongah gets itchy feet and feels restless, like a cat or moonstruck dog, sooner or later.

But he is home today, reclining on the bashed-up sofa that lies humbly outside on the small porch as though grateful for having been rescued from the dump.

'Where ya bin? Call yaself me brother, ya poxy bastard, and as soon as ya cheque comes ya piss off,' Charley cries genially.

'Never do,' Floyd sulks.

'Hah! Where's a price, then?' Charley retorts.

'What, ya think I'm made of money?' his young brother complains.

'Yeah', Charley grins, 'the rate you steal.'

Floyd grins, too, and surreptitiously pulls out a ten dollar note.

'Get a carton, what you reckon?'

'Nuh, get two,' Charley chuckles and pulls out a twenty. He yells over his shoulder for two of the younger boys to go and get the drink, then turns to Doug.

'Ow was the old 'eartbreak 'otel, Dougo? Full of shit, eh?'

'Good food, though,' Doug smiles.

'Might be goin' to Meeka next week,' Charley says to Floyd. 'See Mum. That new bloke she's got now beat 'er black and blue. I'll make 'im piss when I catch up with 'im.'

'Well, Mum like to run away from a good bloke like Digby. I could of told 'er that bastard Paris 'ud use 'er up. All them Windy's the same, look,' Floyd retorts.

The brothers talk about the proposed trip to Meekatharra. They could get a gun off uncle Peter Stone and shoot a few roos for a change of diet from the pies and pizzas and chicken dinners and fish and chips they eat in the city. A bush person hungers for a bit of red, dripping meat after a while. Besides, it will be good to get back into the wild, hot heart of their real home.

Doug feels alone here with all the screaming, crying, laughing Davey clan, whose members are all so much darker than he. He is not black enough to become a real part of the secret, shy world around him, the world that bore his father then cast him out and only nursed his children with uneasy hands. Yet neither is he white enough to become a part of the busy scurrying race that rushes along like a perpetual mice plague, getting into everything and leaving behind a stale smell.

He has no desire to 'get somewhere'. His sister Jemima has got somewhere by marrying a rich young farmer from the district in which they grew up. His brother may have got somewhere if he had not been killed. Two out of three is good enough, he thinks. He wants to lie back and look at Nature's wordless stories pictured in the beauty of the moon, a huge tree or a frail flower. Just as his ancestors had sung and swung in rhythmic motion with the breeze and clouds and rolling rivers, so will he sing praises to the marvels of life and make up his own legends.

The beer arrives and everyone gathers around begging for a drink. Charley sits supreme and at peace, brushing younger brothers and sisters and cousins away as though they were flies.

He rocks his little son upon his knee and feeds him the odd sip of beer. Start them off young, then they won't feel the bump so much when it comes as they get older.

The baby gurgles happily and reaches out to his uncle Floyd's face. Floyd laughs joyously and pretends to cringe away from the little hands. He plays hide and seek, ducking behind a chair and appearing again suddenly, much to the baby's delight.

The little hands grab Doug's long hair and pull so the brothers laugh at Doug's pretended pain and he is brought into their circle again.

'Ya wanna go to Meeka, Doug? Plenty of yorgas up there, mate. Meekatharra womans rock like a rattlesnake, unna, Floyd?' Charley chuckles.

'Sure,' Floyd grins and looks at Valerie, who glares back.

'Let Moira Johnson try and grab ya down 'ere and see what she gets,' she growls.

'Moira Johnson? 'Oo's Moira Johnson?' Floyd asks in mock surprise, trying to suppress his smile.

'You know bloody well 'Oo,' Valerie says.

'Moira Johnson and the rest, too,' smiles Charley. 'Can't forget them pretty things.'

They all guffaw while Valerie leaps on a laughing Floyd, who is too weak in his boundless mirth to defend himself from her playful punches.

Doug is off in a drink-induced dream again and can only raise a half smile. He hardly notices Polly sitting down beside him until her fingers creep up his stomach.

'What ya thinkin' about now, ya funny ole bastard? Ya always off in ya own world, unna?'

'Well I was thinkin' of us two and when I get rich.' He smiles into her open, contented face.

'Ya better not be thinkin' of another woman. Me and my sister the same blood, ya know.' She points with her lips towards Floyd and Valerie, who are rolling around on the dirty, scabby, lawn, having fallen from the verandah.

'Let's wrestle in our own style,' he murmurs and pulls her to him.

'Tchoo, shame, Dougie. Too much people 'ere,' she giggles.

'No shame if yar in true love, Nana,' he whispers and they kiss on the steps. Floyd, covered in grass and dust, just like Valerie, nudges him cheerfully as he goes up the stairs after his romp.

Look 'ere. Properly married, or what? 'Ow ya goin', Daddy Dooligan?'

'OK, Granddad Davey,' Doug grins, and they all laugh once again.

What a magnificent day it is, thinks Doug. Relaxing in the sun, with the best girl in Perth beside him and drinking the coldest, nicest beer he has had for ages. All friends around, enjoying the laughter and talk and sunshine and drink together. Charley's woman, a shy dark wongi from Kalgoorlie, comes out and takes the baby, fearful that drunk Charley might drop him. After she puts the baby to bed, she comes and has a quiet drink with her man.

Another two cartons are bought and drunk. The younger Daveys scatter, like cheeky whistling parrots darting through the treetops, into town or over to the cubby hideout that is their own secret. The white boys here might have their bikes and radios or stereograms and other nice things but only the Davey tribe has a four-room underground cubby, with a fireplace even, where they can sneak off to smoke or drink or try out new girls.

Floyd and Charley's Nanny comes around with a carload of relatives and three flagons of wine.

Drunk talk now. Talk of being brothers forever and never fighting each other and just you wait until I catch that Florrie Snow, the big shot bitch. 'I'm a Davey, and you're my grandson. A Davey don't back from *nooo*-one, boy.' ''Oo are you, anyways? Doug Dooligan? Why, of course. Ya old Carey's boy, unna. Me and Carey good mates; best fuckin' mate ya can 'ave, old Carey', . . . and so on and so on.

Doug just sits and drinks slowly, sharing his cans with Polly. He has never really trusted Chinese-eyed Bevan Palmer, who has a permanent scowl and cold, vicious eyes. That's what too much jail can do to a man, too; boil him up as if he is an apple being stewed in a stone cauldron, until he is all shrivelled and sour inside.

Any of the three fat Stone brothers who are perched like unsteady crows on the verandah railing might turn angry at a wrong word and they're all big heavy men: killers and all.

A shiny black panel van glides into the kerb at the front of the house and silence descends upon the dark group. It stands like a pedigree exhibit, a car above cars.

Silver climbs out of the passenger door and stares apprehensively up at the verandah.

'Oo's that?' scowls Bevan.

'Silver. Ya know, Sylvester Jackson,' Floyd answers.

'Not Jimmy Jackson's kid?' one of the Stones asks.

'Gawd. Could that thing 'ave a kid, could it? Fuckin' miserable old toad 'e turned out to be,' hoots Nanny. ''E used to foller any woman around. Anything with tits 'e'd grab' she cackles while the boys try to shut her up.

'Hey, Pretty Boy! Me and me mate here brought a charge,' Silver calls.

'So what's it doin', 'avin' a baby?' Gary Stone calls back. 'Come up 'ere, brother. We ain't ignorant.'

'Ya got any wadgula womans in the back, mate? 'Amlet 'ere particular about white womans, ya see.'

Roddy Stone grins whilst Hamlet, the youngest and quietest brother, blushes.

Silver's mate turns out to be another white boy who might well have been his brother. He has the same amount of tattooing and the same brilliant red hair, anyway.

They walk self-consciously up the path, aware of the dark watchful stares. They sit down on the bottom step and Silver passes up the flagons of Brandivino and sweet muscat to increase the collection squatting on the dusty floorboards.

Silver introduces his friend as John Williams, known to his acquaintances as Shagger.

Shagger squints around with watery green eyes to see if there are any dark flowers to pick, but it seems that all the girls here are spoken for. He flickers away from Nanny's shrewd gaze, looks at Charley and Bevan and reminds himself to behave with these two around.

Silver is quiet today and ignores Doug, except for furtive glances every now and then.

Gradually, as the nyoongahs grow used to the strangers, the talk and laughter resume. Shagger works as a mechanic and sometimes plays football for the Railways, a south-west football team, so the talk is about cars and football players and teams.

In the middle of laughter at one of Hamlet's jokes, Silver beckons to Doug.

'Come here, Doug. I want a word with you, alone like.'

Doug stumbles down the steps, ignoring Polly's warning hand

and not seeing the Davey brothers' sharp looks at each other, or Shagger's hard, questing gaze.

The two youths wander down the path.

'Yeah?' mutters Doug. He doesn't mean it to come out aggressively but it does, so he kicks a can out of the way and looks across the road.

On the verandah everybody waits for a fight. Floyd has told them all about last night, elaborating as he always does, spinning out an exciting story, with slender, yellow fingers and the magic of his tongue making a silver web to catch all the juicy flies and hold their interest a moment or two.

'Well . . . last night . . . ' Silver mumbles, then blurts out, 'Well, anyway, I'm just really sorry. It was a cunt of a thing for me to do anyway, you know, and I'm real sorry, Doug.'

A slow smile spreads over Doug's surprised face. He is surprised because Silver has never said 'sorry' to anyone, and it must have taken a lot for him to do so now.

'No worries, broh,' he mutters. 'My fault too. I was drunk last night and I'm sorry, too, for pullin' a knife on ya, Silver.'

He holds out a hand and Silver takes it gladly. 'Brothers for ever and ever,' Doug smiles.

The lopsided fence posts, half eaten away by white ants, the scruffy weeds and the brand new, arrogant panel van all witness their sworn love.

Later on, as it gets dark they move inside and decide to play cards for money. Floyd lends Doug some money so he can join in the fun.

They drink, they drink. Shagger foolishly pulls out a wallet full of notes. He agrees to buy them all a feed and some more beer and lets Charley, Floyd, Doug, Silver and Hamlet come for a spin in his pride and joy, so they are happy with him tonight. Shagger thinks of all the girls these boys will know and smiles to himself lecherously.

They return as the sun is sinking into the ocean behind the jagged city. Another day is dead and gone, shattering red clouds across the sky like a broken beer bottle. What will tomorrow bring?

Shagger screeches up to the tired old fence, his machine contemptuously spitting grey sand from its rear wheels. The young men fall out and split the sky with their raucous laughter. Arms wrap around shoulders and they troop up the path.

Doug slumps down beside Polly and cuddles her closely to his thin body. Not even eighteen months of three square meals a day and hours in the gym have built him up. Polly smiles softly at him.

''Ave fun, Dougie? We could 'ear youse mob from way back.'

'Good car, all right, Nana. What ya reckon we buy a car like that, when I get rich?'

Floyd chuckles from the shadow.

'Wishin', Dougie. But she is a pretty machine.'

'I wouldn't mind a GTX,' Charley says.

'I wouldn't mind a charge,' Hamlet calls.

'Yeah, well, ask Shagger, 'Amlet, ya bony thing. 'E bought it, anyways.'

'Sit 'ere, Shagger. Don' be frighten of us *black* Ab'rig'nals. We not goin' to eat ya.' Floyd chuckles and grabs his woman who screams and laughs at the same time.

'Not unless ya turn into a big red kangaroo, mate. Fuckin' spear ya then,' Hamlet grins.

'Right up ya 'ole,' agrees Charley.

'Make you 'op then, unna?' cackles Floyd, so Hamlet laughs too and chokes on the flagon of wine he is drinking. In his coughing he nearly falls off the verandahs. The sight of legs and arms flailing the air and Hamlet's surprised whoop sends them all into fits of laughter again.

Shagger drinks for a while with the youths on the front verandah, then ambles inside to play cards. Two more cars have since pulled in; most of Floyd's aunts have come around to catch Nanny and the remains of her pension cheque.

The young women eye Shagger with sly amused eyes while the older women gaze at him coldly. They know him and his kind; they've been off with some bunji man grinding into them for a few dollars, not caring about them, when they've been as drunk as judges. All the men except Bevan and the Stone boys watch him speculatively, but they ease him into the conversation and make him feel at home because he has his pay cheque on him and a nice car.

Out on the verandah the younger men drink and play Charlie Pride on the battered old tape. Hamlet plays the guitar.

Silver's woman, Rebecca, comes along with two girlfriends and the party livens up even more. Charley, a serene smile on his lips, falls asleep, warm and at ease with his woman beside him.

Once or twice, police cruise past in their blue or white cars and stare in at the rowdy, happy crowd.

Doug's eyes begin to close and he sips beer or wine mechanically. Polly nuzzles into his neck.

'What's up, Dougie? Ya bin sittin' quiet like a mouse, all night nearly.' Her dark lips brush against his ear and she whispers seductively, ' Ya wanna go to bed, Dougie?'

Bleary eyes look into her roguish ones.

'Yeah. Why not?' He grins drunkenly and they stand up to go.

'Where are ya goin', Doug?' Hamlet shouts.

'We're off to see the wizard, the won'erful wizard of Oz,' Doug slurs while his woman supports him.

'Polly'll give you wizard, boy,' cries Valerie gleefully.

'Give 'er an 'idin', Doug. She never 'ad one for ages,' suggests Floyd.

'She never 'ad one other thing for ages, too,' crows Rebecca from beside Silver.

'Tchooo, that's shame, Rebecca,' chides Floyd.

Doug and Polly slip into a darkened bedroom and lie down on one of the many mattresses lying around there.

'Eat ya 'eart out, baby,' Doug cackles.

'No worries, Kojak Dooligan.'

'Nuh, I'm the Incredible 'Ulk.'

She titters.

'Let's see ya turn green, then.'

'Might frighten ya off and we can't 'ave that,' grins Doug.

He runs bony fingers through her unruly hair and draws her musky odour and her beery breath and the remnants of yesterday's perfume deep into his lungs. He sinks his teeth into her neck and gives her a love-bite so that she moans in ecstasy.

Tonight she thought there would be a brawl when Silver came around. She was afraid for skinny Doug as he stumbled down the path and into the murky darkness, and not altogether trusting when he and Silver came back after their muted conversation. He is such a strange boy, she thinks; he hardly ever talks and his smile is so sad. She wants to look after him and give him the something he is missing and searching for so desperately if she can. For he is searching and he is desperate. Despite her tender years and her lack of schooling, Polly Yarrup is a woman through and through and can sense, with a woman's intuition, the frustrations and fears and triumphs raging in her man's soul.

'Dougie, ole darlin', ya goin' to marry me?' she ask.

'Mmm? We'll get married in the best fuckin' church in the country,' he mouths. 'Flowers an' all for my baby. Organ playin' hymns and every kind of thing, yeah. Doug Dooligan's ya man, yeah. Biggest crim in country.'

'Aaah, you talkin' drunk, now,' she mutters sadly. 'Anyways, ya not a crim. That's all over now.'

'It's all over now, Baby Blue,' Doug sings and laughs quietly to himself, then hugs her round body in his stringy arms.

'Polly-wolly-doodle all the day,' he sings again in a husky voice, then kisses her all over the face and neck and breast while she cries softly with all her spirit for him to take her.

They both think it is the best lovemaking they have ever experienced; not out loud, like a rooster crowing at the death of gentle night and all her warm secrets, but soaring silently in circles of inner joy like a godly eagle, swift and high above earthly matters.

Against the guffawing, rowdy drunks, ready any moment to break into a fight, against the arguing card players and the yelling sick babies and exasperated mothers, they make their drunken, violent yet tender love on the creaking bed. All the world belongs to them, for they are all the world they want.

That night, Gary and Roddy Stone stagger about the room arm in arm, talking genially about raping Polly until Floyd pushes them angrily outside to sleep in the car. Bevan has a brawl with Shagger after accusing him of cheating at cards. Then Charley wakes up and, to protect his house, he tries to stop the fight, so he and Bevan fight on the front lawn. Hamlet crawls away and is violently sick, then takes one of Polly's cousin's friends to find a sandy patch in the pines.

But Doug sleeps peacefully, not even hearing Pretty Boy and Valerie making subdued love in the bed opposite. In his dreams he is someone again, always with demure Polly by his side.

Next day is Sunday. Doug wakes early, wondering for a moment where he is, then he smiles at the sleeping Polly, remembering. He feels really good, despite the drinking last night.

He climbs carefully out of bed, leaving Polly asleep and ambles out into the passageway, dodging various bodies slumped on the floor, as well as sheets of last week's paper, bundles of dirty clothes and used nappies and cigarette butts. He scratches himself lazily and wanders into the kitchen in the hope of finding a scrap to eat.

Floyd lounges in one of the chairs, chewing thoughtfully on a piece of toast.

'G'day Doug. 'Ave a good night?' He winks cheerfully.

'Not too bad.'

'Ya missed out on one fight 'ere last night, buddy. Bevan and that wadgula bloke 'ad a cruel rip, right through the 'ouse and into the back there. Ya c'n still see the blood, look,' and he points to the line of blood spattered over the peeling blue paint of the wall.

'Shagger give Bevan a pretty punch, right 'ere, look.' He points to his jaw. 'Then it was on. Charley give 'em both only three punches, jab, jab, jab go his knobbly fists 'and put *their* lights out. Charley got scared for the kid, but, see, and ya know, when Bevan gets tempered up, ya can't stop 'im.' His eyes gleam as he relives the most exciting thing to have happened to him recently.

'Ya want a feed, buddy? Eggs in the fridge there, if ya like,' he offers.

Doug busies himself cooking a feed while Pretty Boy's nimble fingers roll a cigarette.

'Tell ya what, Dougie brother.' Dark eyes dart into grey, a sanctuary where no one needs secrets. 'Valerie 'avin' my baby. What ya reckon of that?' He smiles like a child with a new toy, yet there is a bewildered look about his usually cunning and composed face.

'That's great, Pretty Boy,' says Doug. 'I'm really 'appy for you and Valerie.'

'Well, don't get too 'appy for Valerie,' Floyd growls mock angrily, and they burst into suppressed giggles.

'If it's a boy, Doug, ya know what I'm goin' to call 'im?' Floyd says earnestly. 'Floyd Douglas Davey, after you, 'cos ya me best friend.'

'Naw, naw. Don' do that. Most likely 'e'll turn out like me. Fuckin' jailbird, or what?'

'No, listen, Doug. That's 'is name, me and Val said last night. And ya goin' to be godfather too.'

'I never been a godfather before,' Doug muses slowly. 'I'd be honoured, Floyd, to be godfather to ya baby.'

'Well, you're me best mate, Doug. I've known ya for a long time now; four years, unna?'

Floyd smiles, remembering. 'I come up and asked ya for a light when you was outside that nightclub, and there we were mates. Funny, unna, 'ow ya make friends. Friends are funny, anyways. I mean, me and Silver is friends, but we fight all the time, ya know? But you and me, Doug, we 'ardly ever fight. We can talk to each other, you know. I can tell you things that bother me and ya can always seem to work 'em out, ya know. I'd hurt myself if you was killed, Doug, I like ya that much.'

A brown hand clasps the creamy arm. 'True, bud.'

'Yeah, Pretty Boy,' agrees Doug. 'We 'ad some fun together. But looks like soon we'll be married mens, unna?'

'Gettin' old, ain't it,' Floyd shakes his hands and puts a quaver into his voice. 'S'cuse me, please, but ya got Pretty Boy Davey 'is pretty pension cheque?'

They cackle in glee until Nanny's wrinkled indignant face glares from a pile of blankets.

'Can't youse sleep, or what? It's only seven-a-bloody-clock in the morning. Git outside if you want to talk.'

So they grab their eggs and toast and amble outside past more moaning bodies. Floyd mutters something about it not being *her* house but his brothers', but he does not say it too loudly because Nanny has the Davey temper too.

The sun sails as gentle as Cupid in a lukewarm sky, shooting golden arrows of love into everything; dogs romp around in the park, children run and shout with laughter and birds cry out joyously from the softly swaying trees.

'Nice day. I wouldn't take a million dollars to be dead on a day like this,' Doug murmurs.

'Let's get Charley's football and go and 'ave a kick,' Floyd suddenly says.

'Oooh, too sick.'

'This'll fix ya up. Get some fesh air into ya lungs, buddy. Come on.'

So Doug reluctantly follows a clowning Floyd down to the park, which is cool and green forever. Shadows creep back like soundless spirits towards the tree trunks, while the sun marches resolutely forwards.

Soon from the watching trees and sky resounds the thud of bare foot against leather, Floyd's loud boasting and laughter from the pair of them if they kick badly or mark poorly.

If Floyd can do one thing better than to steal, it is to play football. When he was a child at school and every time he goes to Riverbank, the teachers and officers remark on his incredible skill and dashing style. He can pluck the ball from the air as easily as Eve plucked the fruit of temptation. He can drop kick, punt, torpedo or screw kick with uncanny accuracy. He can tackle and hardly be tackled and handball as well as Polly Farmer used to, some say.

Yet he has never got anywhere, just as his bull-shouldered brother has never become the boxer of renown he should be. Being in a team means being tied down to rules and regulations, and time wraps chains around you with training sessions and other demands. This is something, that, with few exceptions, the freedom loving Aboriginals cannot understand or handle, though they avidly follow sport and envy those who make it in that area.

But Floyd still enjoys himself, kicking an old balding football around with friends. He shouts out, 'The man 'oo couldn't play football, Mr Floyd Davey,' then turns to the trees and bows, 'Thank you, thank you.'

It must be the one time he is really and truly alive, as he sails towards the sky, as graceful as a swan; a black swan, the souls of his ancestors that float on the river named after them.

Doug wishes he can find that kind of joy himself as he clumsily falls on the ground, miskicks or chases after the elusive, bounding ball. Perhaps the closest he has ever come to it was when he worked in the prison garden and his own lean fingers made the flowers grow so that he felt like someone special.

From the darkness of the pine plantation hobbles Hamlet, his tousle-haired woman behind him.

'Jesus, I'm sick as a dog. Gimme a Nummery, for Chrissakes!' he hawks and spits.

He sprawls back on the ground and smokes his cigarette; he is already old, even though he is only about twenty, with wrinkled face and the shakes and red-rimmed eyes. He becomes interested in the two youths kicking the football around, so rises shakily and joins in. But he misses an easy mark and falls flat on his stomach so he has to stumble away and vomit behind a tree while Doug and Floyd laugh happily. Soon, they, too, may be like that, old before their time, but today it doesn't seem possible.

In dribs and drabs the others crawl from the house and are drawn towards the worship of the little brown leather god that sails high in the air. Soon they are all out there in various stages of recovery and undress, the men pretending to be famous football players, tumbling and kicking and wrestling and guffawing with the fun of it all, safe in their own little world. The women gather under the shade with the babies and tease their men.

Only Bevan sits apart, vicious and sullen, until he decides to walk home on his own, where no-one knows of his shame at being knocked out with only two punches. His eyes, as angry as coals, burn into Charley's broad back, but he dismisses the idea of a fight. Charley drunk and Charley sober are two different people, so he goes home.

Doug gets hot and goes to sit with his woman. They giggle and squeeze one another and kiss under the Moreton Bay fig trees that leap from the earth like ancient warriors, dressed in all their green finery.

'What a peaceful day, Polly. I wish days like this would never end,' he tells her, looking into her friendly brown eyes. 'Did I ever tell ya that I love ya?'

'Tell me again.' she returns, soft as the shadows, and they unite in another beautiful young kiss.

Valerie grins across at them then yelps as Floyd's fingers close around her neck.

'Get away, Floyd Davey. Ya scared shit out of me then', she complains.

'I'll *beat* shit outa ya directly.' Floyd grins and nuzzles her.

'Oh, up ya arse. I'd make ya piss, anyways.'

'Come on, then,' Floyd chuckles, and they start sparring.

Valerie Yarrup is the only one of all Floyd's girlfriends who knows when to tease him and when to leave him with his moods and temper. That is why they get on so well, and why Floyd looks after her like an old mother hen, especially now, since he knows she is pregnant. So he lets her small yellow fists pummel his body while he sends laughter up to the sun.

All he can understand is fighting. While Polly adores Doug for his gentle fingers and quiet words, Valerie admires Floyd's flashing fists and prowess as a street fighter. Floyd can only just comprehend Doug's peacefulness. Deep down, though, he is afraid of Doug, for twice now he has seen the scrawny youth's temper rise.

When the two finish romping and are panting on the ground, Floyd's dark eyes stare over at Doug. He appears to be relaxed, yet his body has a tautness that puzzles Floyd. Sometimes there is a restlessness in his grey eyes that only shows when he thinks no-one is watching.

'Hey, brother,' calls Doug.

Floyd jumps self-consciously, realising that Doug has seen him watching.

'Got a smoke for me and my wife?' Doug asks.

'I'll be bridesmaid at ya wedding,' giggles Valerie.

'I'll buy the ring,' Floyd says.

'Why? What's wrong with ya old one?' Polly grins cheekily. 'Too much boys go through ya in Riverbank?'

'Hey, don' talk dirty.' Floyd sulks, while the girls titter.

At lunchtime, everyone pools their money and they buy a big feed of chips and chicken and bottles of Coke. They lie around in the sun, sleeping and talking about the things of their world; feuds, women, babies, who has died, and who has been born.

Doug must go. He should have been home on Friday night and now it is almost Sunday night. It has been a lovely weekend except for the fight on Friday night, but in the back of Doug's mind has been the thought of his mother worrying and that has spoilt everything a little.

He, Floyd and the Yarrup sisters walk to the bus stop. As it grews darker it becomes colder and windier. Icy little elves tug at the quartet's hair and brush it over their faces.

'Did ya see Silver?' Valerie remembers, while Polly's face crumples in laughter.

'Nuh. Where'd 'e get to?' Floyd asks.

'E was sleepin' in the garden. Up the back, amongst all them weeds, with Rebecca,' Valerie cackles. 'An' ya know what? They was both naked like babies.'

'Truly?' roars Floyd happily. 'Ooh no, that's shame, unna, Doug?'

'Everyone goin' to the toilet could see 'em. Two brown eyes winkin' up at them,' Polly remarks.

Floyd cackles like an old crone.

'No wonder 'e never come down with the others. You wait'll I see 'im tonight. I'll tease 'im wicked.'

Doug wishes he could stay too. Still, there is next week. Dole cheque week.

So he climbs on the bus, feeling lonely and waves goodbye to Polly and the rest.

He arrives home at about eight o'clock and knocks timidly on the door, which is opened almost immediately.

'Oh,' his mother greets him in a tired voice, 'It's you, is it? Have you run out of money at last, and had to come home?'

'No,' he sulks, already feeling an argument in the air. 'I come 'ome to see you. I was at Charley Davey's house all day,' he feels he has to add.

'With Floyd?'

'Yeah, 'course.'

He feels foolish, standing out in the cold darkness. When they first moved into this house he felt he belonged, but, as first Carey then Jemima left, he too wanted to move.

'Well, Doug, I'm about ready to give up. You haven't changed at all, you know. I think I'll ring up Mr Salvadorez on Monday and tell him I can't handle you, so you may as well go back to jail.'

'What ya mean, go back to jail? I done nothin' wrong,' he cries. 'Jesus, I just go to see my friends and I'm in trouble. We never stole anything, ya know. We was drinkin' and playin' cards and playin' football today.'

'There's no need to shout, Doug. You and your father are the same. Thinking that shouting wins arguments.'

'Well, you started this argument, ya know. I open the door and what do I get? 'Hullo Doug, how are you? Did you have a good weekend?' No way. 'Oh, it's you!', he mimics. 'That's what *I* get.'

His mother hugs herself and stares into his defiant face with worried eyes.

'Come on in, Doug,' she says.

He comes in, squeezing past her. She has lost him again — perhaps she never found him, not in all his life.

'I've got you a part-time job, Douglas, just across the road, at those stables.'

He stares at her, his cloudy eyes brightening.

'Yeah?'

She smiles.

'You remember Mr Foley, who owns all those trotters? Well, he saw you moping around the house last week and came and offered you a job. You start on Monday at seven o'clock; cleaning up the stables mostly, I think it will be. You only work in the mornings and I don't see why the Social Security should know about it.'

'Ya becomin' as big a crim as me, Mum,' Doug whoops, then he recalls Floyd's present and pulls out the necklace. It winks wickedly in the light of the flickering TV.

'Floyd gave ya this present, Mum.'

'Oh,' she smiles wryly, 'and who did he steal this from?'

'No-one,' he says indignantly, slipping like a platypus back into his waterhole of dark dreams and remote, separate existence.

He doesn't emerge all night and sits silently watching the Sunday movie. He does, however, make her a cup of coffee, showing in his own way that he and his mother are still friends.

That night he thinks of Polly and Floyd and Floyd's baby. He wonders if Polly will have a baby. He could live with her and a baby would be nice; something he could hold in his hands that was prettier, by far, than any bouquet of flowers he has ever grown and picked. A part of him.

Floyd surely is a lucky person.

He thinks of his job tomorrow and chuckles softly. Things aren't so bad after all. With the extra money he earns, he will really have some fun with Polly.

6

Mr Foley is a short, solid man. A good man. He and his stables have been in East Perth since time immemorial, or so it seems. People come and people go, but Mr Foley is always there, getting greyer and greyer. His immense stables glower over the little hovels that clutter these streets of downtown Perth.

Doug's mother wakes him up early, before the sun is fully dressed in all its daytime splendour. Birds chirp and whistle in Edith's garden. These are the sounds he relishes as he chews on toast and gulps down some milk.

He smiles happily at his mother and touches her gently.

'I never thanked ya last night for the job, Mum. It was good of ya to get it.'

'Well, you always got on with Mr Foley and he likes you.'

He can remember the long talks he and Mr Foley have had about horses and racing and trotters and jockeys, an exciting world.

He wanders over the road and into the stables where he rolls a lean cigarette and squats against the wall, catching what sun he can. Right now the men are out riding the spiders around the streets before too much traffic comes. The clip, clip of the trotters on the bitumen and the squeaking of the spiders are sounds he has grown to know and enjoy.

Soon a heavy-set young man comes in. Doug eyes him warily, but he has the Foley look about him and the Foley friendliness.

'G'day, champ. You must be Doug, eh? I'm Tony Foley.'

A huge paw engulfs Doug's hand. 'Like horses, do you?'

'Yeah. On the farm we 'ad a few,' says Doug.

'That's good. Can't have a bloke who's afraid of horses. The work's pretty easy, really. We just need to tidy the place up a bit. We're thinking of selling out, see. To a bloody nightclub, can you believe it?'

Tony Foley's eyes rove around the stately old buildings. 'It'll be a shame to sell this old place. I've quite liked it here. I grew up here you know, playing in these same old stables.'

He sighs. 'Oh well, enough gabbing. Got to get these yards fixed.'

So Doug begins working.

He respects the Foleys who, if they even know, don't say anything about his turbulent past. He spends the mornings cleaning the stables and heaving bags of grain or bales of hay around. He helps Tony fix the grey old pole fences of the four yards and every now and then he gets a chance to help the two reinsmen clean down the trotters.

The horses are indeed fine creatures with satin bodies and eyes often as wild as the horses of Mars must have been. There is nothing more elegant than a fine horse, thinks Doug.

Every Friday he goes down to the dole office where he feels as small and cringing as a worm, with all the other people in a cesspool of poverty and inadequacy. Every Friday he also goes to visit Mr Salvadorez, whom he trusts a little more after each meeting. He is just a man with worried eyes and a wistful smile who gets loaded with all the misfits of society. With the patience and love of a Swiss watchmaker, he mends them and gets them ticking again. Doug opens out about his friend's misfortunes and lifestyles and Mr Salvadorez does listen to him and offers suggestions about how they can better their ways, such as going to youth centres and hostels run by the nyoongah children themselves, where they make their own rules.

Doug surprises Mr Salvadorez. When he can talk to him in the stuffy little office, the boy's eyes brighten and his hands flutter like birds as he expresses his thoughts. The parole officer is pleased that his words are getting through to the frail boy, who, through one moment of foolishness, has ended up on the other side of the table.

For two weeks Doug works in the most wonderful world he has known since he left the farm. He loves the sour smell of sweating horses and the sweet smell of fresh hay, scents that seem so strange with the concrete city only twenty minutes' walk away.

Then there are the smoke-ohs, with everyone gathering inside the musky old stable and old Foley bringing out steaming mugs of tea. The stoop-shouldered, squinty-eyed reinsmen and Tony and the old man all make Doug more welcome than he has ever felt before. They talk about horses and who's going to win what race and about other trainers. The talk is as soft as the swishing rain that patters lightly outside upon the fresh green tips of this year's batch of weeds and upon the backs of this year's winners. For, with the passing of May and the advancement of June, the days get colder and the rain begins.

But it cannot last forever.

On his second Friday there, after gleaning several sure-fire tips from the stables' crew, Doug decides to try his luck at the trots.

It seems that the horses he backs are as swift as Pluto's phaeton and that he has the luck of the devil himself. Amidst the glaring lights, roaming people and chanting bookmakers, he makes five hundred dollars.

He gives his mother a hundred when he arrives home, weary and happy.

'Tomorrow I might go and see Floyd, Mum. I also want to see Polly.'

He has told her about Polly. She is happy for him, of course, but she cannot appreciate his love. She has never seen Polly and Doug decides, then and there, to bring her home; then he really will be rich.

'Look after yourself, Douglas. You're being such a good worker for Mr Foley and it would be a shame to spoil it all now. Try not to get too drunk, won't you?'

'No worries, Mum,' he assures her.

The next morning he catches a taxi to Valerie's flat in Balga, feeling flash with two hundred and fifty dollars tucked away in pockets and socks.

It is a grey, sullen day with a threat of rain. Nothing can dampen Doug's spirits, though.

A cautious Valerie opens the door and smiles weakly at him.

'Dougie; 'day, mate. Floyd's gone off stealin' again, the useless, silly prick,' she cries. ''E don't care one bit for this kid. I may as well jump off the Narrows Bridge.'

'Naw, don't talk silly, Valerie. I got some boya, look. I won at the races,' he says gently.

'Ya could buy some food then, Dougie? Us mob 'ere are cruel starvin' for a feed.'

She lets him past and he crowds into the passage. He can smell her musky overnight scent and stale food and the sickly, sweet red wine that someone has spilled. This is his world.

Valerie follows him into the sitting-room and notices that he gazes at the fresh blood all over the wall.

'Yeah. That's that silly bugger Floyd again, goin' stupid,' she complains. 'Honest to God, I dunno why I stick with 'im. 'E got blue drunk last night and got to thinkin' I never loved 'im, so 'e smashed a stubby over 'is own 'ead and blood come out like water, true's God. Then 'im and Silver took off stealin' and I never seen them since.'

She turns around, exasperated. 'The monaych can eat 'em for breakfast for all I care now.'

She hobbles over to the door of the bedroom, calling, 'Polly, ya man 'ere to see ya.'

Doug sits down sadly. Every time he comes here, something has to go wrong. Poor Floyd, so young and unable to express himself in any way except through violence — even to express love, the tenderest yet cruellest of emotions.

Polly blunders through the doorway and smiles languidly, sleepily.

'Long time no see, darlin',' she mutters, then snuggles down beside him, gazing into his face in adoration. 'Bloody Floyd kept us awake all night with 'is muckin' about. Tchoo. I screamed when he hit himself. I thought 'e was dead, true,' she whispers, awestruck.

'I dunno what we're goin' to do about this flat. It's shame, ya know, when all those white people stare at ya, every time ya get out in the sun.'

She shivers and huddles to her man for warmth. 'Jesus, I'm hungry. I could do with a big juicy chook and lots of lovely, lovely chips.'

'Unna?' Doug smiles. 'Big, bad Doug'll look after ya!' A sly hand snakes into a pocket and he pulls out four twenties coiled like orange creatures ready to spring out and grab some fun.

'Da daah!' he crows.

'Dougie,' she breathes and stares into his happy face. 'Ya been stealin'?'

'Nothin' like it,' he cries indignantly. 'I got a job now, 'oney. Besides, I was at the trots last night and got on a lucky streak.'

'That's good, 'cos Dougie,' she murmurs, cuddling up close to him again. 'If you go stealin' and so on, I'm leavin' ya straight out. I don't want no man in and out of jail all the time.'

'You an' me Polly-wolly-doodle all the day.'

'Ahh shut up, ya silly ole bugger,' she giggles, and they chuckle together.

'Tell ya what,' Doug announces, 'You, me and Valerie'll go to one picture. One Vampire picture'll scare ya into next week.'

'Oh, yeah. I never been to the pictures for a long time.' She claps her hands joyously and gets up to tell sour Valerie the good news.

The girls shower and dress in readiness for town, while Doug idly shuffles cards and practises the tricks that Micky Connelly taught him in jail.

Then they leave in a taxi, since only the best will do for the affluent Doug Dooligan.

The rain whips around their stringy bodies as they alight from the taxi.

Doug feels really great walking beside the two giggling girls, like a great chieftain walking through his concrete jungle, instead of a useless part-Aboriginal who has been lucky for once and who may never be so again.

They buy a feed at Brown's milk bar, then go to the Railway Hotel across the road and play pool and drink a few slow middies to while away the time. When they first walk in, the barmaid looks at them dubiously but then she sees Doug's roll and lets them pass. As long as they are well-behaved, it's all right.

The movie is a good one: periods of quiet are interspersed with sudden flashes of terror that make the audience scream and the Yarrup sisters both clutch Doug, giggling with fear. Even Doug glances around once or twice with prickling scalp, expecting a vampire to rush at his exposed neck, jaws slavering and eyes white-hot with lust for blood.

Out in the sun and normality again, the three laugh at each others' fright and share a cigarette in the mall.

Heavy black clouds crouch on the tops of grey buildings like strange birds of prey. They will swoop down at any moment and tear someone away from the slippery streets with cold, wet talons; up into the mountainous sky where their hungry young wait in soft, white nests.

People stare at Doug, Polly and Valerie as they crouch on a seat smoking and giggling.

They decide to walk to Gary's.

The rain has started. The wet, miserable streets are darkening now. The three feel safe in the green world with its twinkling, clattering occupants lined up along the wall. The jukebox, queen of this world, has her throne in the middle against the wall. She hulks, silver and blue flashing and her servants come to pay penance, twenty cents a time, so she will howl her lies like a dog to the moon. The foolish people believe and smile and dance and listen.

Painted women, with eternal smiles, and bold buccaneers or grim space heroes, all gaze down from the pin ball machines' backdrops, like trapped spirits tempting the boys from the streets to waltz with them through time and space and become a part of the machine for a brief second.

It is Saturday night, so Gary's is quite full. Two dead-eyed sailors sit hunched over a game of Space Invaders, killing aliens in the same way as they kill time, and being blown redly all over the screen when they make a mistake. A group of white children cluster around the racing car set in the corner. Some Aboriginal girls sit around the middle pillar playing pool and listening to the jukebox.

Doug's young cousin Maureen Greyboy, resplendent in silken, shimmering purple disco pants, sidles up to him.

Give us a loan of a dollar, Dougie,' she wheedles.

'Nuh, carn do it.' He smiles at her dejected face. 'Can only give ya five dollars, Maureen.'

Which he does, pulling it out of his sock.

Unlike all her brothers, Maureen Greyboy is quiet as an innocent lamb, but she is not innocent. She has already turned fifteen and she was blessed with the good looks of her mother before drink and boys got her at the reserve like hungry foxes.

'You hear about my man, Willice, Dougie? Poxy judge give 'im six months just because 'e stole a blanket.'

'Fuck that,' he murmurs in sympathy. 'Judge must of 'ad shit on 'is liver that day, unna?'

'Willice never been to Freo before,' she moans.

Doug knows how Willice will be feeling. He wraps an arm around the morbid Maureen.

''E'll be right, cousin mine. 'E'll only do four months, anyways. Go and see 'im if ya like and cheer 'im up.'

A smile flutters over her pale brown face.

Valerie, Polly and Doug play pool and listen to the music while the night creeps in over the hills, from the forests of Mundaring and the fields of York.

They wander outside and it's raining. The sighing of the rain tries to coax Doug's thoughts back into his old world, where he used to sit under a dripping tree and watch the wonders of Nature through a misty, fairy haze. Then there was just Doug Dooligan and his land, and every tree and bush and flower belonged to him as well as the secret things, like kangaroo nests in the reeds on the salt flat, the birds' nests in trees and the wild bees' nests full of sweet honey, and possum trees covered in scratches and with a hole full of warm bodies to catch.

Not any more. He has caught a warm, brown, big-eyed body, with tangled blonde hair and a gentle smile like the morning sun. The only nests he knows now are hidden rolls of money in arrogant houses, or food in stores — sweeter by far than the honey he used to rob. The kangaroos here are wily and dirty and loud and they hop from detention centre to detention centre, never escaping the great white hunter.

Valerie nudges a dreaming Doug.

'Nylers just went past. A red GTX.'

They fade into the shadows of an alley and nervously light cigarettes.

'Let's go 'ome,' Valerie says.

'It's only eight o'clock,' Polly complains.

'Listen, those Nylers know I'm goin' with Floyd. Ya want me to get a floggin'?'

'We'll go 'ome to my place,' Doug says, to stop an argument that may bring the police if it continues. 'Then when it gets dark, we'll get a taxi to Balga.'

'Suits me,' grins Polly, hugging onto his arm, and Valerie agrees reluctantly.

They walk out of the alley, straight into Jenny Campton and her cronies.

'Doug!' she cries and stands facing him, hands on fat hips. Her murky eyes glare at little Polly, who shrinks into Doug's uncertain protection.

Jenny Campton is drunk on wine, as she nearly always is nowadays. She cannot comprehend Doug, whom she has loved and still does. She often dreams of him in her drunken stupors or when other men — black, white or in between — grind her into the dust. Yet he doesn't love her, and she wonders why. Out at the camp they told her he was going with another girl, a Yarrup.

That makes it worse because the Yarrup clan, though small, is from the lower south-west and are therefore the natural enemies of many Perth nyoongahs. Jenny has vowed to her mates that she will fix Doug's slut properly, just wait and see.

'Ya fuckin' bastard, Doug, leavin' me like a cunt. I'll make ya fart, ya poor skinny little *shit*,' she yells, bringing people pouring from Gary's.

'Go away, Jenny. 'Ave a bit of sense, will ya?' Doug hisses as his eyes dart around for a means of escape. But all Jenny's solid, glowering companions have fenced off the alley.

'Ya leave me like that, unna?' she cries and snaps her fingers. 'Ya too good for me now — is that it, ya 'ot-shot criminal? Ya prick too good for my tuppy?' she screams so the crowd laughs softly and Doug hangs his blushing head, wishing he could disappear through the ground.

Little Polly shoulders Doug aside and scowls into Jenny's mocking, ravaged face.

'Don't talk to my man like that, ya dirty mouth bitch. 'E wouldn't go with you in a fit, ya so ugly. Us Peringrup girls are the prettiest in the State. That's 'ow come we get all the best men,' she crows.

Jenny comes in swinging. Her first punch knocks Doug down so he sails back and crashes into the rubbish bins.

Then the fight is on. Valerie joins in when Jenny kicks her sister, shouting for a fair fight. Then Jenny's mates join in, while the yelping, laughing crowd swirls around the mouth of the alley, heads bobbing to get a good look at the brawl. If they're lucky, the girls might tear their clothes, so the boys will get a glimpse of something nicer than a fight.

Doug recovers and stumbles out of the shadows to try and break up the fight. Jenny kicks him in the groin, so he retches and falls back into the crowd. Arms encircle him and hold him up.

He hears Tiny's cheerful roar: 'Bugger me, where'd you spring from, Dougie?'

'My woman . . .' he gasps.

'Let 'em go, let 'em go,' Tiny laughs.

Then a shout from the back of the crowd informs everyone that the police are coming, so, like a covey of doves, they flutter and scatter to all four winds.

When the CIB car and the van pull up, Gary's is deserted except for a few people (and they are all white). In the alleyway only a lonely blue thong remains. Baffled again, the detectives cruise around town, searching for a clue, but all the dark, shiftless youths are hidden in their alleyways and vacant blocks, waiting to creep out again later. Even if they do question any Aboriginals, the detectives know they will be greeted with silence and vacant eyes.

'Bloody boongs. You may as well let them all kill each other, then we can all have some peace. They're just bloody animals anyway,' sneers one CIB man to another.

Doug, feeling sick in the stomach, is dragged by Tiny over the William Street bridge into the dark, tattered arms of West Perth. They go through Little Italy, where all the shops have Italian names and Mediterranean-type food, and the clubs are Italian-owned. There are also discreet gambling houses hidden away upstairs.

Tiny gets some money off Doug and buys a small bottle of V.O Port to cheer them up. They slouch into a nearby car park among the drying, dying milkwort plants that stretch their shaggy heads up to the lopsided moon.

'I've got to find Polly, Tiny,' says Doug.

'Wait a minute. Wait and see, Dougo. Don't want the monaych up ya 'ole, do ya?'

'Look, Jenny Campton might grab 'er again. She can't fight.'

'Can she what!' cackles Tiny. 'Brother, she 'ad it all over Jenny Campton.'

'Ooooohh, I feel sick.'

Tiny chuckles and offers the bottle to a sagging Doug.

'So'd I feel sick if I got a kick in the balls.'

'Ya oughta try it one time, Tiny. Does wonders to ya system,' Doug groans and they both laugh, though somewhat feebly.

Laughter takes away the pain of most things. That is why Tiny and so many of the People always laugh, because they have the pain of failure that sometimes becomes too much. Then Tiny will cry. Laughter and tears through all the years. What else are we born for?

Headlights lance across the near-deserted car park and jab into the boys' startled faces. Doug corks the bottle and tosses it under the old ramp, with all the empty bottles and cans of solitary dreamers, while Tiny fumes.

'Damn it! Should of drunk over at the Pier Street crossin', he says. Doors slam. Feet harshly clatter down towards the two youths, not like the possum-quiet pattering of the night people who usually sneak here.

'What do you know? It's our mate, Doug, the big-time brawler,' sneers the huge driver of the Boys from Brazil.

Doug goes cold inside. No-one is around to see what happens: just a few deserted cars and dead bottles and crushed cans and scrawny weeds. There is just the shivering Tiny, who is next to no help at all, since he and Doug are both in the same situation.

'Been drinking, you two?' asks the small, evil man.

Two heads shake.

Whap! A hand slaps Tiny.

'Been drinking?' he asks again, gently.

'Do ya see any fuckin' drink on me, fuck ya?' cries the youth, while Doug cringes, waiting for his turn. What a bloody night this has turned out to be. He could be home in front of the heater watching TV, and yet here he is about to get a hiding, just like his cousin who is being dragged off into the darkest corner.

It is his own choice, though.

'Well, I don't know, Doug. I thought you'd given town a miss since I haven't seen you lately,' a soft voice purrs.

He looks up into the calm eyes of the quiet man, reflected in the light of the quiet moon. Behind him he can hear the other two working Tiny over.

'It's a free world. I can come to town if I want,' he sulks.

'Oh, I'm not stopping you, Doug. Go for you life.'

The man moves closer. 'What were you and your mate up to

tonight? You know anything about that fight?' he shoots out suddenly.

'What fight?'

'This fight.'

The man's hands grab Doug by the hair and pull his face around to the one light that guards the shabby car park, so the gentle glow bathes his face and shows up the bruise Jenny Campton gave him.

'I run into a wall.'

What's the name of the wall?'

''Adrian's wall,' Doug smirks.

'You're so funny, Doug,' the man sighs. 'Well, I tried to be nice to you, because you seem to be intelligent. But you're making it very hard. Do you *want* me to give you a flogging?'

'Try it,' Doug growls, his feral eyes closing to angry slits, 'and I'll get Legal Aid onto ya so fast ya 'ead'll spin. I got rights, ya know. I'm no dumb nigger you can push around.'

'Then why hang around with dumb niggers like this one here?'

''E's my cousin. Ya better leave 'im alone, too.'

He hears Tiny give an animal cry.

'Dougie give me the money, ya cunts.'

Then he hears footsteps coming behind him and a heavy hand spins him around.

'Where's the rest of the money you stole, you black bastard?'

'I never stole nothin',' says Doug.

He is punched in the stomach, just above where Jenny kicked him, so he stumbles and nearly vomits. He screams to the moon and the clouds and the city buildings watching impassively.

'I won it at the fuckin' races!'

He is lifted off his feet.

'I don't like you, Doug,' the driver whispers. 'I'm going to take you down to Central and make you eat shit, you understand? Last time I saw you I told you to call me sir. S.I.R. . . . sir.'

'I won it at the fuckin' races — sir!'

'All right, Doug,' says the quiet man gently. 'We believe you. You don't have to tell the whole town. If we see you or your mate tonight we'll all go for a little ride down to Central, won't we?'

But Doug isn't allowed to go just yet. The burly driver hustles him over against the rusty fence and slams him into it so that both the fence and the boy creak in pain. Maniacal eyes glare into his.

'I hate your guts, you little mixed-blood misfit,' the driver sneers. 'If it's the last thing I do I'm putting you back in Freo, where snivelling gutless snakes like you belong.'

He pushes Doug away. 'Piss off to Tiny, now,' he chuckles. 'You boongs sure get lumbered with some stupid names.' He swaggers back to the waiting car.

The Boys from Brazil back out and it is peaceful once more. A low whistle near the Pier Street crossing tells Doug where his cousin is, so he pickes up the wine bottle and limps over the silent, empty park. His echoing footsteps are the only sound.

Tiny is slumped against the small ticket collector's shed.

'Bastards never even believed my name was Tiny Williams. I can't 'elp bein' born so bloody small that they give me a weird name.'

'Well, 'ave a charge, anyways,' Doug consoles him. 'Need a bit of wine after all that, what ya reckon?'

'If I 'ad a gun I'd shoot that big prick right between the eyes. I'd make 'im and 'is poxy mate fart with that gun, boy. Then I'd cut off 'is balls and make 'im eat them,' Tiny scowls.

So they console themselves with fantasies and red wine, and clutch the shadows to them like sweethearts.

After the bottle is finished, they creep out and head back to town. Outside the old Crystal Palace that has been re-named Timezone they meet Maureen Greyboy, who tells them that the Yarrup sisters started walking for home and that Jenny Campton is still around.

'Screw 'er. She spoiled my whole night,' Doug says angrily, working himself up into a rage.

He and Tiny start to walk towards Tiny's bus stop. Just as they get there, a battered dark car pulls up beside them. A murky face from the window hisses, 'Get in youse two. 'Urry up!'

It is Floyd. He peers over his shoulder with cold eyes and studies Tiny and Doug silently. He's in one of his moods again; better be careful, Doug thinks, and gives Tiny a warning nudge. In the car are Hamlet Stone and two of Bevan Palmer's younger brothers, each of whom has the same cruel Chinese eyes as Bevan.

'So,' Floyd ponders, 'where's my woman, Dougo?'

'Gone 'ome.'

'Yeah. I picked them up, thumbin' a lift. I could of been any old bunji man.'

'Listen, Pretty Boy, after the fight we all split up. Me and Tiny was caught by the demons, unna, Tiny?' says Doug desperately, knowing his odds and sensing the Pretty Boy is drunk and violent and that no-one is a friend.

'Yeah, ya skinny split-arsed yellah bastard,' snarls Floyd. He grabs hold of Doug's shirt, jerking him forwards. 'Whaffor ya go startin' fights? Valerie's budjarrie for me, ya know. If she 'as a miscarriage from tonight's rip, I'll kill you, Doug, true's God. I spit on my dead Dad's grave.'

But Doug is tired of being pushed around tonight and his anger overflows as he cries, 'Let me go, Floyd, before I lose my temper. I never started no fight.'

'Ya want a fight, do ya, Doug? Ya own two womans there, dragged 'er in, and you know that. All my people 'ere, Dougo: you and Tiny'd be 'istory. Ya can bring big 'Ughie for me, too. I'll give 'im a fair go too.' Floyd is working himself into a fighting mood.

'We'll all be 'istory in a moment, if we don't fuck off,' Tiny says calmly. 'Look 'oo's coming down the road.'

A red GTX. The Nyler clan.

Floyd spins around in his seat and revs the motor so the car leaps away from the kerb and screeches around a corner. Floyd's cousins grope for the pieces of iron that roll sluggishly on the floor. Hamlet picks up an empty wine flagon and glances fearfully at the pursuing car.

'They're comin'.' He turns to Doug. 'Ya 'ear what 'appened to Bevan? Nylers caught 'im that Sunday we was at Charley's.

88

Poooh brother, they made 'im jump! 'E's still in 'ospital, ya know.'

Doug wonders just what he is doing here, being shoved from side to side by the motion of the car. Any moment they might get caught and beaten to pulp by the angry dark people in the angry red Holden.

'We'll never lose 'em. We'll 'ead for Millars Cave and fight 'em there,' Floyd calls.

'Plenty of bottles there. Places to run to, too,' adds one of the Palmers.

'If Jimmy Nyler's there, then 'e's mine,' grates the older brother. 'For bootin' Bevan in the balls and face, I'm gunna kill 'im.'

The car screeches around a corner and then skids into Millars Cave, a vacant block by the railway line in East Perth. It is a haven where Aboriginal alcoholics congregate to drink and die. Every now and then the police or City Council move them on, but they always come back to camp underneath the few skinny, dirty trees that have survived the advancement of the white man's city.

Right now a car park is supposed to be going up here and piles of rubble, dumped as filling, offer the escaping boys numerous weapons.

They explode from the car. Someone throws a bottle that smashes against the side of the red GTX. Then the Nylers leap out, swearing and yelling, their voices sharp in the blue emptiness.

Shadows join with shadows; grunts and shouting and cries of pain pierce the clouds. Bottles smash wickedly and gleam in yellow-brown hands as the young warriors set out to avenge all their wrongs.

Pretty Boy's fists knock one enemy down, but Hamlet's blonde head is shattered with a flagon, so he collapses. The youngest Palmer is besieged by two hefty youths and belted all over the place, while the other Palmer boy holds his own against a bottle-wielding man. Little Tiny heaves a brick through the red car's front window.

The howl of sirens whines closer and closer so the boys scatter in every direction. The Nylers tear out of the block in their wrecked car while the others leap over the rusted old fence and race along the tracks, then hurl themselves into the rank weeds along the line. Three cars burst into Millars Cave. The youths keep their heads down while their hearts pound.

The three cars light up the place with spotlights and headlights in an eerie yellow-white glow. Mechanical voices buzz strangely over the intercoms while big-booted policemen run to and fro over the battlefield.

They find nothing.

The wet, stringy grass embraces the youths with the kindness of a mother. Doug licks his bashed-in lip where someone flattened him as he skulked by the side of the car, trying to keep out of the fight. Beside him, young Hamlet holds his blood-soaked head and moans softly. Floyd peers over the weeds with alert black eyes like a chicken-stealing fox.

'They'll be around 'ere in a minute.'

'That's the Boys from Brazil, over there.'

'Fuck that, then. Let's get out of 'ere.'

Doug feels sick in the stomach. All he needs now is to be caught again by the three CIB men. Obviously Floyd stole that poor miserable wreck of a car over which the police grope like spiders.

One by one the youths rustle away, crawling along on their bellies until they come to the Claisebrook station just up the way. They huddle in the shadows of the deserted building and pull out cigarettes.

'Ya see Jimmy Nyler jump? I told ya I'd make 'im koomph.'

'Poor bugger 'Amlet. Collected the lot, unna? Orta get 'im to 'ospital.'

''Ow was Tiny, eh? You should of 'it that big jerk Billy Nyler instead of 'is poxy car, but.'

'What was Darryl Johnson doin' there? I thought 'e was our cousin?'

'That little wall-eyed prick! 'E's 'istory if I catch 'im. E'll be playin' 'is 'arp,' Floyd snarls.

Doug leans into the shadows and pulls his coat around him so he doesn't get cold. All they can ever talk about with any enjoyment is fighting or women. Only occasionally will Floyd surprise them with his philosophies of life. They don't comprehend the larger issues of this world. They are born and they die and the biggest thing to happen to them is an all-out brawl with the Nylers or some other enemy.

Even Doug is caught up in their world when he could go on to far greater things. What is he doing standing in the shadows, in the dribbling rain, waiting for the police to tear into them with sharp white lights and loud voices, and maybe hard fists? Who is beside him? His diminutive cousin, the angry Palmers, a sorry Hamlet and the arrogant, drunk Floyd. His people.

'Let's clear off out of this before the monaych come.'

'Yeah. Keep to the back streets and keep an eye out for them Nylers.'

Floyd rests a hand on Doug's dejected shoulder and his eyes probe Doug's pondering face.

'See ya tomorrow. Look after yaself, buddy,' Pretty Boy says gently, then he fades away with the other flitting shades and Doug is alone. He squats down and smokes another cigarette. Better wait awhile, he thinks. He has to cut across the East Perth park and cross Wellington Street with all its lights, so he is the one most likely to be seen by the police or the Nylers. He enjoys the murmuring rain and the solitary feeling; he wraps the night around him like a cape and dreams.

The brown CIB car drifts down the road and turns up the way the others went. Doug sees the pale face of the driver and is reminded of what happened earlier.

It's time to go home.

He hunches into his coat and thinks that the next dole cheque can go towards a new one. This old brown coat is ten years old now; first of all it belonged to one of his white cousins, then it was handed down to him.

The desolate winds howl like hungry wolves and groan like their dying prey. All this part of East Perth is dedicated to wrecked cars, in the yards of panel beaters, and wrecked people in alcoholics' homes and the Children's Court. Empty, dirty, collapsing buildings line the narrow rutted streets.

But it is Doug's home, where in a real sense he grew up. These places hold memories for him, so he is not alone as he wanders back to his bed.

7

On Sunday night, when Doug is watching the TV movie, safe and happy with his Mum, there is a timid knock on the front door.

Doug hears muted voices, then his mother comes back, a stony look upon her face.

'It's Floyd. Don't stay out too long now, darling.'

''Course not. I want to watch this movie,' Doug smiles and wanders out to the door. Floyd is standing nervously on the verandah.

''Ullo, brother. Ya comin'?'

'Aw, I dunno. I oughta stay with Mum.'

'Naw, I'm goin' to Meeka t'morrow and I might not be back for ages.'

He leans close to Doug's face. 'Besides, Polly wants to see ya.'

Doug decides to come, as crafty Floyd knew he would. Pretty Boy stands, stamping upon the verandah like a wild, restless stallion, while Doug slinks back inside for his coat.

'I'm just goin' to see my girlfriend, Mum.'

'Oooh, darling,' she answers, disappointed.

'Yeah. Well . . . see ya. I shouldn't be gone long.'

Then he is out in the cold dark world of Pretty Boy.

The car is parked under the ravaged box tree in front of the house. Doug eyes it suspiciously.

'Oo'd ya steal this off?' he asks cautiously as he slides into the back.

'Not stolen,' grins Floyd. 'It's Uncle Peter's, unna, Silver?' he lies so that he does not frighten his friend away.

Silver smirks from the front seat.

'Long time since I saw you, Dougo, man,' he laughs. 'You turning over a new leaf, or something?'

'Might be 'e's turnin' over a new woman,' Floyd chuckles, slamming the front door and revving the engine.

Doug catches a glimpse of his mother, peering out the front window and for a brief moment he wishes he was still with her. Then he is hurled backwards as the car bounds away. Floyd yells happily, while Silver offers him a half-empty flagon and his feeling of regret disappears. You only live once after all, he thinks, and you might as well live with your friends.

'Ya got any money, my brother?' Pretty Boy smiles.

'Give us a smoke, Dougie. I've run out here,' Silver says.

They drive around the near-deserted city block, seeing if there are any girls or mates to whom they can show off. Floyd's deft hands caress the tatty wheel of the car that he owns for the night.

Silver lies back, half drunk, like a complacent cat. He has just spent a most successful week with his mate Shagger, visiting a number of white hippy ladies, breaking into several houses and smoking lots of Shagger's dope. His blue eyes are half closed in contentment. What more could a guy ask of life? And next week, for two bags of the best grass in Western Australia, Billy Todd will put a new tattoo on his thigh — and won't *that* be a sight for the girls to see?

'Poxy town is as dead as a doornail,' Floyd complains.

'You two are married men, anyway. I don't know why you're looking for tarts,' murmurs Silver.

'You just wait till Rebecca catches you, ya double-dealin' ole bull,' grins Floyd. He changes the subject. 'Last night was too pretty, eh Dougie? You got clobbered, any rate.'

'Yeah,' Doug breathes ruefully. ''Ow's 'Amlet?'

'Oh, 'e'll survive. No one could touch this nyoongah 'ere, but.'

94

'Fighting's stupid,' Silver says, which brings a cackle to Pretty Boy's lips, for Silver Jackson is the biggest brawler around when he isn't relaxed and stoned.

They drive home to Balga.

Doug goes up the stairs again, the stairs that know his footsteps so well now.

Floyd hammers on the door.

Valerie opens it and stares stonily at the beaming youth who pushes past her abruptly and stalks into the living-room.

'G'day, Dougie. Polly be back in a minute. She's just gettin' us a feed.' Valerie sounds tired. She ignores Silver, who ignores her.

'Come 'ere, Dougie, and watch some TV. Vincent Price on later,' Floyd calls, truly lord of the manor.

Last night, when he took the sisters home, he had an argument with Valerie over stealing. In his drunken rage he slapped her across the face and punched her so hard that she cried. Now he pretends it never happened, because deep in his heart he is greatly ashamed, but it has never been in his nature to apologise.

They watch TV.

Valerie stands by the door, watching and waiting. When her man came in at four o'clock in the morning, cold and miserable and drunk and dog tired, she forgot the night before and held him in warm arms like the baby he sometimes is. But the very next night he is out stealing again.

Polly comes in, laden with fish and chips; Doug gets up to help her, while Silver guffaws and Floyd eyes him mockingly.

Out in the kitchen, he holds her close to him.

'Sorry about last night. About leavin' ya and the fight and all. I tried to find ya after but monaych pulled me and Tiny up, ya know.'

She smiles serenely into his troubled grey eyes.

'It's orright, Dougie. Ya backed me up, didn't ya?' Her small fingers brush against his lip, bruised from the night before. 'Poor ole Dougie. Can't get away, can ya, budda?' she croons.

'It's nothin',' he tells her.

95

'I really miss ya, Doug. Why can't ya stay 'ere?' she urges.

'Carn do it, Nana. I gotta work now.'

'Yeah,' she muses. 'Well, I could stay at your place, then.'

They kiss and wish the kiss would last forever.

They return to the living-room. Floyd crows, 'Well and about time too. Youse two aren't married yet, ya know. We run a respectable 'ouse 'ere. Kissin' and cuddlin' and all this carryin' on, *I* don't know.

'I'm just practisin' for the big day,' Doug smiles and flops down on the sofa, pulling Polly beside him.

'I wish my woman would let me practise on her.' Floyd pretends to sulk, which is the closest he will get to telling Valerie: sorry about hitting you and running out on you and stealing all the time. But just try to see the good things about me.

Valerie, who knows her man, accepts and coils up beside him, wrapping an arm around his elegant neck.

They immerse their minds in the flickering TV, talking every once in a while. Rebecca ambles home and she and Silver disappear into the bedroom, ready for a night of argument or love.

At last Floyd rises and stretches hugely.

'Better get ya 'ome, Dougo. You gotta work t'morrow and get us lots of lovely boya.'

'Don't you stay out too late, Floyd Davey,' Valerie warns, 'or ya might just find one girl gone from 'ere.'

'That's OK,' Floyd grins. 'Me and Silver'll make a move to Cleo's then.'

'Blood'll run in the streets if I catch you lovin' it up with those Freo sluts at that nightclub,' Valerie warns and Floyd laughs genially.

Floyd is quiet on the way back to East Perth, nursing his stolen car gently and lovingly, just as Doug nurses Polly in the back seat.

They pull up in the dark, deserted street outside Doug's house. Pretty Boy stays mute for a few moments, staring out at the fluttering box tree and into his own thoughts. Doug can see that he wants to say something, so he asks Polly to wait under the verandah and lights her a cigarette.

Then the two youths are alone.

'Tell ya what, Dougie,' Floyd says, gazing after Polly's retreating body. 'Ya one lucky man to get a woman like that. She not too pretty, like some I know, but she's good to ya. She don't run around behind ya back, ya know.

'You and me, both: we're lucky men,' he ruminates, then turns to look Doug squarely in the eyes.

'I mess up everything, Dougie, true's God. I 'it Valerie right in the stomach last night and I could kill 'er baby, God knows. Why do I do somphin' like that?'

Doug pats him gently on the arm.

'It's not your fault, Pretty Boy. Everyone loses their temper. That's what wars are all about. Valerie still likes you, that's the thing. Ya seen 'er tonight — all over ya, and you the biggest thief goin' when ya get in the mood. No matter ya belt 'er, Floyd, she still come back to you. That's true love. That's somphin' to cherish.'

'But why'd I 'it 'er for? And then I even wanted to fight you, Dougie, and you somphin' special, budda. You like my own brother.'

'Fuck this temper,' Floyd cries in anguish. 'Fuck the drink, too, 'cos it destroys everything good in a man, ya know?'

Doug hugs him, murmuring condolences.

'Sometimes,' Floyd says calmly, 'I feel life just ain't worth a cent, and I may as well end it all. Bein' alive sure is a funny thing. Ya'd think it'd be one long party, unna, with all the good things around, but it's a fuckin' waste of time, more often.'

He holds out a hand. 'Look after yaself, good buddy. See ya when I come back from Meekatharra.'

'You look after ya own self, too, Pretty Boy,' says Doug.

Floyd's great hand clings tightly to Doug's bony wrist just as a dying man will clutch at a straw. They shake hands.

'I love ya, Dougo, like I dunno what. Ya can love 'orses and cars and girls. But I love you too, ya know. You and me, all the way: forever and ever, mate,' he says earnestly.

Then, as silent as a thought, he and his car cruise away and

Doug is clattering up the stairs to his waiting woman. He drags her, giggling, into his little room with the bed that is desperate for young, warm, intertwined bodies.

Meanwhile, Floyd has driven the car around the corner. At the lights, winking wicked red and full of warning, a police car noses up beside him, and two faces peer in at him. When he turns, so do they; they keep on his tail all the way up the hill. He feels as a rabbit must feel when the shadow of the eagle far above falls on its quivering body. His anxious brain works overtime as he drives slowly, hoping they will pass.

They don't. More lights.

He turns again. When they follow, he suddenly bursts into life, putting his foot down, fishtailing across the slippery road, then dodging around another corner. His speedy takeoff has fooled the police car for a few vital seconds, but that is all he needs. As the police dash around the corner in pursuit, Floyd's lanky body springs from the car that has careered up on to the kerb. He hurls himself over a fence; rolling along the ground on the other side, he hears the police car's doors slam and authoritative shouts. Then he is doubled over, running through the darkened garden and vaulting another fence, hoping there are no dogs. Like lightning, he flashes out of the second garden, across the road and over the wasteland of the East Perth park towards the safety of West Perth.

Not five hundred yards away, Doug holds his woman in gentle arms and promises always to love her.

That is why, at seven o'clock in the morning, instead of his mother waking him up with a kindly shaking of his shoulder, there is a pounding that shakes the flimsy door. Doug opens the door, scratching his stomach and rubbing the sleep from his eyes.

Two detectives, as real as the rising sun stand there. Short hair, clipped moustaches, neat suits, shiny shoes and the sort of eyes that all detectives seem to have; probing, cold, and invariably blue.

'Huh, y-yeah?' stammers Doug, taken off guard.

'Douglas Dooligan?'

'Yeah.'

'I'm Detective-Sergeant Conway and this is Detective Stevens.'

'Yeah.'

'Do you mind if we have a look around your room?'

'Why?' he hisses. 'Can't you mob ever leave me alone?'

Cool eyes rip into him.

'We'll leave you alone if you tread on the right side of the law, Douglas. But you're not doing that so much, just at the moment, are you?' the Detective-Sergeant says quietly.

'What ya mean?'

He is shouldered aside and the two men walk in, picking at his few possessions and fingering them so that he has no privacy at all.

'Who's the sleeping beauty, then?' Detective Stevens murmurs.

'Wake her up. She was in on this, too,' Conway orders.

'In on what?' Doug flusters.

'Douglas,' the man says sadly. He holds up the watch that Floyd gave him almost three weeks ago. 'I'm surprised that you should steal this watch. It's not your style, old mate. It just goes to show you can never comprehend the criminal mind.'

'Look, I never stole bugger all,' Doug says, fully awake and afraid, and wishing his Mum would come. She probably doesn't know I'm here, he thinks despondently, the way I took off last night, but perhaps she heard the knocking.

'Rise and shine, sweetheart,' he hears Detective Stevens say.

Polly's eyes open wide in terror for a few seconds, then they blank out.

''Oo are you, wakin' me up at sun-up? Can't a person get any sleep any-fuckin'-where?' she snarls to hide her fear.

'Have a late night, did you, darling? Where were you when your boyfriend stole the car last night? Keeping watch on some street corner, I'll bet,' the Detective-Sergeant says rudely.

'Go on,' she mocks. 'Me and 'im was 'ere all the time.'

'What car?' asks a confused Doug.

'Douglas must have been too interested in lover-girl here to see what car he stole,' says Stevens attempting sarcasm.

'Well, let's remind him. A green HK, Douglas. You haven't got much taste, have you?'

He sees the momentary flicker of recognition in Doug's eyes.

''Aaaah,' he says, 'that one'. You can't have stolen too many cars, Douglas. Tell us all about it.'

'But that . . . that's . . .' he stammers.

'Yes?'

'That's not true,' he finishes lamely, thinking of Floyd and his ''Uncle Peter's car''.

'Of course it is. Your fingerprints are all over the seat and the door,' Detective Stevens says.

A heavy hand encircles his skinny arm.

'Come on, Douglas. You're under arrest. Come quietly and make it easier for yourself.'

'What ya takin' Dougie for? 'E done nothin',' Polly breaks out of her silent cocoon.

'What did you say your name was?' the Detective-Sergeant says, with his wonderful knack of hearing yet ignoring.

'It's Polly Dawson.'

'How old are you, Polly?'

'I'm sixteen,' she lies again.

'Sure?'

'No, I'm an 'undred and twenty-bloody-one,' she snarls.

'You carry your age well,' Conway says mildly. 'But that's good, because Doug is in a lot of trouble now, what with stealing cars and watches. All he needs is a charge of carnal knowledge to top it all off.'

Carnal knowledge. There they were, making what they thought was beautiful love, and all along it was just 'carnal knowledge'. People have to spoil everything. Doug chokes.

Polly sits up in bed, angry and desperate for her man.

'Ya can't be told, unna? 'E never stole no car.'

'Who did, then? Do you know?'

'Nuh,' she says, sullenly.

'No, I'm sure you don't. Come along then, Douglas.'

He is hustled outside. He moves along in his 'given-up' shuffle.

'Can I see Mum?' he asks.

'Your girlfriend will tell her all the necessary facts, I'm sure,' the Detective-Sergeant says, as he pushes Doug into the sleek, smooth Kingswood.

Detectives' cars seem so impersonal, with their clean vinyl seats and neat carpets. They even smell different from other cars; perpetually new. And Doug, who likes old things and disorder and darkness above everything else, is hopelessly lost. He cringes in a corner and sniffs sadly and thinks of jail again.

He hasn't even been out a bloody month. He certainly does walk a thin tightrope these days.

'OK, Doug,' Conway murmurs from beside him, 'make it easy for yourself and spill the beans. Why, I'll bet you only get a fine, with your parole officer there to speak up for you.'

The youth looks with dead eyes, into the smiling face, then away again to the tears trickling down the window and the children running in the rain, so free.

'You've got yourself a nice piece of crumpet there, Dougie. Be a pity to lose her, don't you think, so soon after getting out of jail?'

Conway leans close to Doug's face. 'I'll throw the book at you if you don't start talking, Dougie, and I do so detest violence. It's so obscene and it makes us look like proper bastards.'

He sighs and leans back, as they cruise beneath the arc of the police headquarters and pull up outside the huge glasshouse that is the CIB building.

Strange that a building with so much glass and light is often the place of foul, dark subversion, thinks Doug as he is hurried through the back door and into a softly humming lift.

Up and up they go, stopping to let more detectives in or out. Some of them wish Doug's captors a cheery good morning and eye Doug indifferently.

Only one comments, 'What's up today, Bob?'

101

'Oh, nothing out of the ordinary. Couple of Abos messing about with stolen cars,' shrugs Conway.

They go into a room that is furnished with a polished desk covered in all sorts of pieces of paper that must be important, Doug thinks. There is also an iron cabinet.

'Now, sit down, Douglas, and let's have a little chat,' Conway says genially. He pushes Doug into a swivel chair, while he himself perches on the desk top, dangerously close to Doug. Stevens stands, his legs astride, and his back to the closed door.

Doug has nearly died in the lift. He thought that any moment the Boys from Brazil would lumber in, and then where would he be? Even now, they might come in. This detective might be their mate. He waits for them to come and work him over, like they said they would only two nights ago. This is their lair, after all.

Doug's nerves are in a jangle.

'I want a lawyer,' he croaks. The Detective-Sergeant chuckles, 'Do you now, Doug? Well, that would be a waste of time.'

'I've been beaten up before, ya know. I never come down in yesterday's rain. Polly'll tell anyone I never 'ad no bruises on me when I come 'ere,' he bursts out.

'And she'd be the most likely to know, you lucky man,' Conway smiles. His eyes probe Doug's face. 'Now listen, Dougie, I don't feel like beating anyone up. Have *I* ever beaten you up?' he asks earnestly, 'or Detective Stevens here?'

Doug looks up cautiously and tries to work out if the expression on the older man's face is genuinely sincere.

'No,' he mutters.

'However, you don't leave here until you *do* tell us what you know, Doug. If you won't tell us, you might tell Detective Maxwell.'

''Oo's 'e supposed to be? The bloody public executioner?' Doug tries to sound defiant.

'You don't know him? Oh, Doug, he knows you very well. He was talking about you only the other night. A big bloke. With a moustache. Drives two other men around. I'm afraid he doesn't like you much at all, Doug.'

Conway's piercing eyes dig into Doug's frightened mind, for he is frightened. He remembers the cruel words of the Boys' driver and the huge fists and big boots and all the damage they could do.

So he tells the truth, and while the words creep hesitantly from his mouth, Floyd whoops and shouts on his way to Meekatharra in his brother's car and Silver rolls in drugged Utopia, with yet another girl in some other house in the intestines of the city.

After the clicketty-clack of the typewriter has stencilled his words, Doug is taken down to the desk in the next building to be charged. He feels as dead as a once-young tree that has been ring-barked; and a tree that now has a dead, grey heart.

He remembers Pretty Boy's gentle and sincere words of last night and feels almost like crying. He is such a coward. But no, not really. He is an artist: a sensitive, lost person, who just wants to live in peace. But at the cost of his friends?

Down in the busy anteroom his mother awaits him. He cannot bring himself to look at her.

She woke late and hurried out to fetch her son for work. In his room, two surprises greeted her: a tearful girl and the news that her son was in CIB headquarters once again.

'Darling,' she says to him now, 'Are you all right?'

'Mum,' he stammers. 'Mum, I never stole no car, Mum.'

She touches him quickly.

'I've got you out on bail, darling. We'll go home and get you a shower and make you presentable for court at ten o'clock. We'll ring Mr Salvadorez. I'm sure it was all a mistake, Douglas. I mean, you've got a good job and everything,' she chirps away desperately. Then adds, 'Polly's out in the car as well.'

But all the birds have flown away now and he stands stark and bare in his grief.

Out in the car he scarcely acknowledges Polly. He slumps into the familiar seat.

'Oh, fuck,' he sighs and turns his back on everyone, staring out the window.

Yet in the end it is not as bad as he has thought it will be.

Mr Salvadorez, with all his fine words, and the Legal Aid lawyer, with all his official phrases, and the judge, in a good mood, get him a six month good behaviour bond on top of his parole sentence and a stern warning that if he ever comes before the court again he will face heavy penalties.

He is not happy, though. He does not feel like going to work so he spends the rest of the ruined day with Polly, drinking his mother's endless cups of coffee and trying to find some enjoyment in the present. The future holds no prospect of pleasure. He keeps thinking of Pretty Boy and what will happen when the police catch up with him.

The noble dreams he had when he came out of prison seem far away and lost now. Prison is like smoke, clinging to one's clothes with tenacious fingers and never letting go. People see the way he walks and look into his eyes and know. The police know and they never forget.

Polly watches with wide, sad eyes. She has seen another side to her man today, caught up in the cruel machine of law and order that grinds people's pride to nothing. She has seen him afraid and confused and not the tough person he makes out he is at all on the streets and in the flat when he is drunk.

But, she thinks, he has never really been tough at all, this frail, gentle youth she loves. He is quite different from the fiery Pretty Boy and the malevolent Silver. In his own way he is stronger than the two put together.

She touches him on the arm and when his troubled eyes look up, she smiles calmly.

'It's orright, Dougie. I'm glad ya got off. We never knew it was stolen.'

His mother's eyes eat away at him and all the ornaments leer down at him like crows on a barbed wire fence. He doesn't belong here, so he grabs Polly's hand and gets up.

'Goin' for a walk,' he says.

'Don't you go near Floyd, Doug,' his mother warns as he and Polly scurry out the door.

They go to the park just down the road. Not Queens Gardens

104

with its self-important ducks wandering around and its stately swans floating around on the stagnant pond; with its fine manicured gardens, and children playing on its neat, green lawns and with its statue of Peter Pan, eternally young. Doug and Polly go to the lonely little park next to the Gardens, with its few Moreton Bay fig trees erupting like green volcanoes from the ground. Doug lies among the roots of the biggest and noblest one, and his dreamy eyes gaze up into the sky. The huge trees look like the billowing sails of magic ships about to sail off into the sky. The picture relaxes him as he leans against the roughness of the tree trunk.

Polly, sensing that he wants to keep his thoughts to himself, silently lights a cigarette for them both and hands one to him. He catchs her fingers and runs a calloused thumb over her palm. He still has her, at any rate, he thinks; she is all that counts.

'Poor ole Dougie, you been worryin' all day. Jail must of really 'urt you, unna,' she consoles him softly and runs fingers through his tangles of wild, russet hair. 'I'd 'ate to go to Bandyup. Niandi worse enough. But you free now, my man,' and she kisses him with honey lips, on the cheek. He hugs her tightly and watches the trees — everlasting and so alive in the wind.

8

The next day when he goes to work for the Foleys, he can feel their eyes brushing his back all morning. Smoke-oh is a strained affair.

The next day also, Silver is picked up as he lounges in Gary's pool parlour. They give him a hard time down at the station.

All that week Doug works; gradually the hay smells and the horse smells and the horse talk lure him back into feeling somebody again. At night or in the afternoon he works in his mother's modest garden, or walks with Polly along the foreshore of the river that meanders through the city. You can tell the river your secret thoughts, your problems and stories. The soft lapping of the water on the weathered old stone walls might be songs from sweet mermaids far away. They lure two more young lovers into their world of peace and love and quiet laughing.

On the afternoon of dole cheque day, just as he is finishing up at the Foley's, Doug receives a visit.

He is fixing up one of the broken poles on a fence, watched curiously by a benign roan horse, when he hears a sharp whistle.

It is not Pretty Boy. It is his cousin, Hughie Tarriot, a skinny, pockmarked young man, with unruly curly black hair, and eyes like black, hard pebbles.

''Ughie? What ya doin'?' Doug asks, and goes over to the fence that runs along the street.

'Gimme a smoke, Doug,' Hughie rasps and hunches even

lower into the coat that is so ludicrously big and new that it can only be stolen. He lights up and eyes his young cousin.

'So, ya workin' now?'

'Yeah,' Doug says proudly, 'I got a good job 'ere.'

'No worries, eh?'

'Nuh.' Doug pulls his own coat around him in the same motion as Hughie. Doug wonders what Hughie wants; his scrounging cousin always wants something when he emerges from the shadows. Otherwise no-one ever hears of him. Then he remembers his mother saying that Hughie has been in Bunbury Regional.

'When did ya get out, 'Ughie?'

'I never.' His cousin smiles mirthlessly. 'I'm on the run, Doug, since today. Me and Uncle Dobie and ya Dad.'

'Dad?' Doug mouths, stunned.

'Yep. They done a stupid thing, puttin' all our fambly together, unna? Still, couldn't 'elp it, could they, what with cousins and brothers every-fuckin'-where.'

Hughie grins without humour. Nothing cheers up this wizened young man, unless it's a good fight or a full flagon.

'Anyways, kiddo, we're campin' just up the road, in them big block of flats, ya know?'

He jerks a thumb towards the rearing tenements at the top of Forrest Avenue, ironically named Eastside Gardens.

'Come up and see ya Dad,' he invites him.

'Don't feel like it,' Doug mutters darkly.

A clawlike hand reaches over the fence and pulls Doug to him suddenly. The black eyes go murky.

'Watch yaself, kiddo. That's yer own Dad there. You never come to see him at Guildford Park, not once. Ya too ashamed, unna? And the way 'e used to carry on about 'is only son. Ya too good now, is that it?'

'Pah,' Hughie spits, 'you and me are the same, Doug. Assaulters, the both of us. You and me don't owe the world bugger all.'

He lets go; Doug staggers back as Hughie hunches once more into his coat.

107

'Come up and see ya Dad t'night,' he repeats. 'Second door along from the lifts on the third floor. Bring ya woman — if she's not too ashamed of sou'-west Abos.'

Doug isn't surprised about Hughie knowing of his girlfriend. What an Aboriginal doesn't know about his people isn't worth knowing about anyway. Even a snivelly, sullen quartercaste has a trace of the splendid powers that enabled his ancestors to converse with people thousands of miles away, or to bone someone, or to sing someone to death or a woman to love.

Hughie slouches off and Doug turns to see big Tony Foley watching him questioningly from the stable doors. He goes back to work apologetically, feeling as though he has been caught out doing something vile instead of just talking to his cousin.

That night he makes up a lie about taking Polly to the pictures. He and she set off for town then double back around the block, thus coming to the flats.

'Where we goin'?' she asks him.

'To see my Dad.'

'Unna?'

They tramp up the stairs and find the place easily enough. Slim Dusty's voice howls through the crack in the door like a watchdog, but shuts off when Doug's nervous tap echoes up the passage.

'Oo's there?' quavers a woman's voice.

'Tell 'Ughie 'is cousin's 'ere,' Doug whispers back and the door is opened. A dumpy young woman stands there while behind skulks Hughie, a big butcher's knife clasped in his bony hand.

In the large room sit several men and women. Empty bottles lie all over the floor or stand against the wall. A young man lies, passed out, on the messy double bed and a mattress on the floor holds four squirming children, aged between one and six years old, all watching a flickering TV set. Someone puts the tape on again, so that blasts away too.

A scattered pack of cards on a blanket, around which the people sit, shows what has been happening today. But now they listen to the tape and sing out of tune to the songs. Or they watch the antics of the TV characters and sing in time to the advertisement jingles. All of them are drunk, for isn't it dole day?

Doug's father Carey Dooligan sits slumped in the corner. His face is an unhealthy yellow and his hair is going a streaky grey. There are so many lines on his face that Doug has not seen before — lines of fatigue and drunkenness and old age.

'Yeah, Dougie?' he croaks. 'Where ya bin? In prison?'

Doug nods, wondering what to say. Hughie nudges him.

'Introduce your woman to 'im, ya ignorant bastard.'

He does and then Hughie introduces all the other people: Krayners from Albany and Wooddins from Gnowangerup and Kenny Barrett from Collie, sprawled over the bed. They are all Floyd's enemies. Doug gives Polly a warning look which she acknowledges. He hopes the Nylers (whose uncles, aunts and cousins these people are) don't come around to help spend Kenny's dole money and recognise him from last Saturday night.

He sits down beside his father and accepts the silently offered flagon. Polly squeezes into the corner beside him, shy and nervous.

'So ya came to see ya ole Dad, did you? Looks a bit of a bloody mess now, don't 'e?' Carey smiles a cracked smile, yellow and broken-toothed. 'Got a smoke on ya, son?'

Doug feels inside his pocket and pulls out three cigarettes. He lights one for himself, hands one to Polly and gives one to his father.

What do you say to someone you haven't seen for almost five years and whom you never really talked to at any time?

The old man's eyes are as vacant as his mind, for all his thoughts have been drowned in the methylated sea that swills around inside his body. The eyes that were once so clear, so soft with simple dreams, are red-lined, half closed and puffy. The pupils appear to merge into the whites so they are a murky brown. His mouth hangs open at one corner like that of a simpleton. There is nothing left in him and nothing left for him.

Yet he has the look of an old warrior boomer, with the mongrel dogs of wasted time and circumstance cornering him and dragging

109

him bloodily to the ground.

'You're a silly old bastard, Dad, goin' to jail at your age,' Doug says.

But he feels pity for his father, who after all sired him and presumably loved him — once.

'We'll 'ave a good drink, Dad,' he says suddenly, and pulls out the twenty dollars he brought with him. He throws it over to Hughie, who lies beside the unheeding Kenny, necking with his new girlfriend, who is a Wooddin and who drove all three escapees here to her flat.

'Where's Uncle Dobie?' Doug asks his cousin Hughie.

'The stupid old tit got stuck into the metho and 'e never 'ad a drink more stronger than coffee for the last four months,' Hughie answers. 'We left 'im 'alf-dead, out at Auntie Deirdre's there. 'Well, what shall I get with this then?' He indicates the money.

'Flagons,' someone suggests and everyone agrees, nodding happily. So Hughie stumbles out to get them.

'Sheep,' Doug's father says, startling him.

'Eh?' he returns, confused.

'Sheep. Me and Dobie shot a sheep to feed Deirdre and the kids and they gave us twelve months. Dobie couldn't 'andle it, but I didn't give a fig.'

'Ya couldn't buy a sheep with ya pension cheque?' Doug asks angrily. Even as he says it, though, he knows that drink and gambling would have eaten his Dad's money away the same day he received it, as surely as the metho is eating away his stomach.

Hughie returns with the flagons and passes them around.

Round and round the mulberry bush, the mulberry bush, the mulberry bush. Round and round the mulberry bush on a cold and frosty morning.

Four plump, red mulberries catch the light from the swinging globe and the fruitflies buzz around and get drunk on the god's elixir.

They are peaceful, singing songs and living old memories and falling asleep. Kenny Barrett wakes up and rolls off the bed,

110

clutching a flagon that nestles like a lover against his threadbare side. Soon he curls up on the floor and sleeps again and no amount of prodding will waken him.

Doug and his father share the same flagon. They try to share old memories, too, but they can only understand the flagon.

Polly sips the offered wine slowly, determined to stay sober and look after her man in case he decides to do something foolish in his inebriated state.

At last Carey falls asleep. Doug, feeling happy and drunk, hugs Polly and mumbles in her ear, 'Me old Dad. I never seen 'im for ages and ages.'

'Well, ya never missed much,' Polly glowers.

'Aaaah, honey. That's my Dad, 'oo I love.'

'Only because ya drunk, Dougie,' she reasons coldly. 'Let's git 'ome before trouble starts. Ya cousin and ya Dad are on the run, ya know. Monaych'll bust this door down and ya finished then, boy.'

'Let me drink with my people,' he says stubbornly.

'Ya people?' she returns harshly. 'These are Nylers' mob, ya winyan fool. They'll rip ya 'ole open in a minute when they 'ear all about you, Dougie Dooligan.'

''Ughie'll look after me. I'm 'is own cousin, look.'

''Ughie's lookin' after 'imself, baby, like 'e always done. 'E's too busy with 'is woman to worry about you,' she whispers angrily.

'Yeah,' Doug grins, 'that gives me a good idea. He clutches her exciting, inviting body close to his and gives her a drunk, wet kiss.

She responds reluctantly, begging him to go home to their own bed. She doesn't like the looks that some of the other men give her. She knows Doug can't fight with his fists and can only use weapons. If he picks up a weapon here, she thinks, all the older men will make mincemeat of him.

Hughie jumps up from the bed, grinning.

'Come on, Doug,' he calls. 'None of that now. We've got business to do.'

111

'What ya mean?'

'You and me are goin' to steal a good car.'

The words sink slowly into Doug's fuddled brain. Then he breathes out long and slowly.

'Get away! I'm not stealin' no car. I just got out of fuckin' court for all that. Steal it yaself; you're the one on the run.'

'I don't know 'ow. You're the car thief in this fambly, Doug. Ya want to see ya poor old Dad back in Freo? 'Cos that's where 'e'll go,' Hughie tells him.

'I never said that.'

'Well,' Hughie says soberly, 'what's stoppin' ya, big brave Doug? I tell ya what, ya not leavin' 'ere unless ya 'otwire a car for me and ya Dad.'

Beside him, Polly can feel Doug's temper rising like a live thing. She holds onto his arms, willing him not to go berserk — not here, please.

'I'm goin' 'ome. Try stoppin' me, 'Ughie, I'll kill ya.'

Hughie throws back his head and bays like a dog.

'Come on then, darling. Come to Uncle,' he crows and dances in towards Doug, who crawls up the wall and comes forward, swaying greatly.

But Hughie is older and has been tonguing his drink all evening. He ducks Doug's clumsy punch and gets him in a head-lock so that Doug is as helpless as a newborn baby. Hughie drags him over to the window and holds him out into the night air.

'Shall I throw ya out the window, cousin-brother? Make a pretty mess for the cleanin' lady t'morrow, unna? Little bits of Doug all over the tarmac,' he laughs cheerfully.

'Let me go,' Doug cries, frightened. 'I'll steal a car for ya then.'

They back away from the window and Doug looks into Polly's reproachful eyes.

'Ya better go 'ome, Polly. Don't let Mum 'ear ya, but, or else she'll want to know where I am.'

The alcohol in him gives him a courage he doesn't really feel.

'I'll be sweet. No worries on me, honey. I'll just get them a car and be right back.'

The cousins lift up a grumbling Carey and half-drag, half-carry him through the door, followed by an apprehensive Polly.

They stumble into the lift while Polly takes the stairs.

'See ya later, baby,' Doug slurs while Hughie hoots at their love.

Polly gives her man a strange, tired look and nods absently.

Down in the street, Doug, Hughie and Carey become part of the shadows. Doug picks up a discarded cigarette packet and extracts the silver paper. He silently twists a piece of wire off a nearby fence. Carey mumbles, asking where he is. Hughie struts along in front, looking out for any roving police cars that might recognise him or Carey.

The moon flits from cloud to cloud like a thief. The cold night air slowly creeps into the nyoongahs' bodies. The noisy warm flat, with its taped songs and hushed conversations, belongs to yesterday now.

An empty backwater street, lined with mauled peppermint trees, cut and hacked about by the City Council workmen until they resemble their tall, graceful cousins from the country in no way at all. Here is where Doug finds the car he decides to steal — a panel van from the eastern States. His sly fingers slide the window down a crack and his wire is slipped in to catch hold of the lock, opening the door.

Now Doug is the boss. He orders the other two into a lane so that their loitering forms won't cause suspicion. Deftly he places the paper over the fuses in the way Floyd taught him. He gives a sharp whistle and the other two scurry out of the lane like rats.

Doug and Hughie heave Carey into the front, then they push start the car until the engine coughs to life. Hughie springs into the driver's seat and Doug hops in beside his Dad, who is asleep again.

'Fuckin' lovely,' Hughie grins and they roar off round a corner.

'We'll take ya 'ome, Dougo; ya done a good job. Then we'll pick up me woman and Uncle Dobie and get out of this rubbishy town.' Hughie nudges his uncle. 'What ya reckon, Uncle Carey? Go and check out those Kings Cross womens over Sydneyside?'

Carey nods stupidly. He doesn't know where he is, what has happened, or even who he is, Doug thinks bitterly.

The meaning of the headlights that reflect in his side window seeps into his confused brain. As Hughie spins around another corner, so do they. It happens again and Doug cries out in panic, 'We're bein' followed, 'Ughie!'

Hughie's sharp face watches the rear vision mirror as he slides into a side street.

'Well, fuck the luck. So we are.' 'Ang onto ya 'at, Doug, 'cos we'll give the bastards a run for their money,' he cries, then they squeal away.

But they cannot lose the car. Doug, peering around once, catches a glimpse of a sleek brown Kingswood and groans.

'The Boys from Brazil,' he says.

'What?' shouts Hughie.

'Nothin', says Doug, but it is everything in his nondescript life. 'This time. This will be the last time; there won't be no more times. Maybe the last time, I don't know . . .' The words from the song whirl through his head.

He bemoans his fate as the car surges forward along the near-deserted streets. He's really put his foot in it this time. What, Dougie, you like jail so much, you can't wait to get back inside? he admonishes himself angrily.

Hughie wrenches the car around a shoulder of the road and nearly runs into the RTA car coming in the opposite direction. He slams on the brakes and the car slides broadside across the road. He wrestles with the steering wheel and they shoot up a small side street, but a blue van comes from the other way, effectively blocking off their escape. Hughie loses control and the stolen van smashes into a picket fence, starting a dog yelping crazily.

Hughie bursts from the van as the police descend upon them. For a split second, Doug is frozen in fear, then, he too, bursts from the lopsided, damaged van, dragging his father after him.

'Run, Dad, run,' he yells, then dodges between two uniformed men and sprints up the road. He hears the huge

Detective Maxwell bellow, 'Hold it right there, you bastards, or I'll shoot.'

Glancing around, he sees the man silhouetted against the street light with a pistol pointed straight at him.

He has never been more afraid in his life. Fear lends him wings and he vaults over a brick fence, then blunders through the busy, weedy garden and clambers over another wall. He trips and falls and rolls away into the weeds in the corner of the garden. On his belly he scuttles along the ground, keeping in the wall's shadows. He comes to some bushes and lies low, while his heart pounds and he waits for the torch to pick him out. Then there will be bullets or fists and back he goes to jail.

He hugs the clammy, sweet soil to his bosom and thoughts of prison, and especially the belting he will get when caught, flash through his mind. Tears of self-pity trickle down his face and he mews in grief and fright.

But back at the jumble of cars and men, Hughie has picked up a jagged picket that he swings at the huge detective, dropping him to his knees. Then he comes in, yelling at the other two detectives, giving the quiet man a glancing blow across the face, before he is tackled from behind.

They slam him against what remains of the fence, but he bounces back fighting and knocks one more of his enemies flying before being subdued with fists and boots and batons.

Detective Maxwell grabs Carey and lifts him off his feet, shaking him like a terrier shakes a rat to death.

'Who was the other one, you filthy old drunk?' he screams in the fury induced by Doug's escape and the blow on his head.

Carey's old eyes look calmly into the enraged face and he spits accurately into the detective's eye.

This is Carey's moment of glory. With all their power they cannot take away the one thing he has: a love for a son as lost as he is. This is what he thinks as they hustle him brutally into the back of the van. He hears Hughie's hoarse cry, 'Pick on someone ya own age, ya fuckin' pigs.' Then the door slams in his face and he is back where he started five years ago.

Doug stays where he is for a long time. Once, he hears a motor bike zoom down the lane with radioed messages bombarding the air. He can smell the bitter scent of the dying tomato bushes amongst which he lies. Their season is almost over but his is just beginning. The police will pick him from the bush and let him stew in prison.

At last he ventures cautiously out and creeps up the lane. He comes out into a street he knows and realises he is only a couple of kilometres from home. He just has to cut across the East Perth park, then up Bennett Street and into Goderich, and he is home. Like a whipped mongrel he slinks from shadow to shadow. Three times he has to go to earth as CIB, RTA or patrol cars crawl past. He wonders if the others got away.

The cold night and light drizzle sober him up. It takes an hour to get home with the roundabout route he follows.

He taps gently on the window of his darkened room and slips inside like a wraith.

Polly's big eyes gaze at him over the sheets while he pants and gets his breath back, for he has run the last bit home. He eases the curtain of the window aside and peeps out.

Stillness.

'We was chased. Christ, am I lucky,' he says to Polly. 'The Boys from Brazil were right up our tails. One pulled a gun on me, Polly,' he says, still shocked at the memory.

She looks at him a moment longer, then turns on her side, to face the grey wall. He slides in to the warm bed beside her.

'I wonder if they caught 'Ughie and Dad?'

'So what! They'll catch ya next time around, don't worry if ya missed out tonight!' Polly cries.

'Sssh, honey. You'll wake up Mum,' Doug warns.

'The way ya use up ya Mum makes me sick! Ya got a nice 'ome 'ere, Dougie, and everything good, and ya *still* gotta fuck around stealin' at night!'

'Be quiet, Polly,' Doug begs.

'No, I won't.' She turns to him, tears glistening in her eyes. 'Them boys just use ya up; ya people use ya up, ya think I don't see that?'

Her voice goes into a whine. 'Gimme a smoke, Doug. Gimme twenty dollars, Doug. Ya my brother, Doug.'

'Fuck ya,' she cries. 'Your Mum's real good to me. I like cleanin' this place up and talkin' to ya Mum.'

She stops and stares angrily at him. 'It's no good tellin' ya, though, Doug. Ya just can't be told. I'm goin' to cry and cry when they take you away. And you Doug? Ya goin' to be laughin' in the back of that monaych's van'or what?'

But she cannot stay angry with this boy for long. He was just going to be another boy she took home for a good time, as she has done before with too many other boys. But this time she cannot leave him. She thinks of him all the time. She feels his joy at working in the stables and laughs at his little jokes and adores his every movement and habit.

'I could really go for a smoke,' Doug says quietly at last.

She lights them each a cigarette and his arm wraps uncertainly around her.

'Cold, unna?' he says hesitantly. 'Bugger drinkin'. I'll never drink again, I feel so sick.'

'If ya never drank, ya never would steal.'

'Yeah.'

'Ya got a good job now, Dougie,' she whispers. 'I dunno what ya gotta go provin' things for. Leave the stealin' to the younger mob, 'cos they only go to Riverbank. But you go to Freo.'

He pulls her to him and kisses her neck and breast. She moans gently and presses against him fervently.

'What ya say to Jenny Campton that time? 'Us Peringrup girls are the prettiest in the State',' he cackles softly. 'Well, that sure ain't no lie.'

He gives her a long and reassuring kiss. 'T'morrow you and me'll go to the pictures. One fillum about a magician bloke, made right 'ere in Perth, they reckon,' he murmurs.

She is all over him, exploring him and loving him. They make love as if it was the first time and they think love will never grow old. It seems to them that they will never grow old either but will stay young and vibrant forever.

9

The next day at smoke-oh, old Foley appraises Doug with thoughtful eyes.

'Having a bit of a rough ride at the present, are you, Doug?'

'What ya mean, Mr Foley?' Doug returns carefully.

'Yesterday that fellah seemed a bit upset. You know, the bloke by the fence.'

'Oh, me cousin. No, no trouble there.'

The Foleys watch him while the two reinsmen pretend not to notice. Doug certainly does feel out of things. These men have worked together for years and not one of them has ever set foot inside his dark world, with robbery and drunkenness and street lights and shiftless street people drifting like leaves from one winter to another.

They go back to work, but the former companionship has faded. Doug works by himself, cleaning out the stables. He can sense doom clouding the horizon.

When he finishes work that afternoon, Polly is waiting for him by the gate.

'Let's go for a walk, Dougie,' she says, and the way she says it warns him of strife.

Down by the river he hears.

'Ya Mum read in the papers about ya Dad and cousin. Ya cousin went mad and didn't 'e tear into them monaych. Someone dobbed Dobie Greyboy in, too. They still lookin' for one

118

bloke — that's you, Dougie. They're goin' to 'urt you, Dougie; no gettin' away from that.'

Seagulls cry into the wind and circle the couple hopefully, looking for a handout.

'No-one 'll dob me in, Polly. That's my people there.'

'Someone always dobs someone in,' she states decisively. 'And ya know what'll 'appen to you, Dougie? Ya'll go up for 'elpin' criminals escape, that's what.'

'Nothin' like it,' he says.

'Everything like it,' she bursts out. 'We oughta get out of 'ere today. We could go to Peringrup and wait till things cool down. Ya can stay with my mob: Mum and Dad and my two little brothers and sometimes Grandpa.'

'No.' he catches her in his arms and hugs her.

'No,' he repeats quietly. 'Tonight I'm takin' you to the pictures, because I said I would. Anyway, I gotta tell Mr Salvadorez.'

'You can write 'im a note.'

'Well, but I got a good job 'ere.'

'Dad can get you a job root-pickin'.'

He brushes tender fingers across her anxious, taut face and smiles the smile she knows and loves.

'Little Polly got all the answers, unna?'

'I've got to, with you too busy playin' silly buggers,' she returns.

That night they shower and dress. Polly borrows one of Doug's sister's dresses since her own clothes are getting dirty now. Then they set off with Doug's mother beaming after them, happy that Doug has found a nice, quiet, sensible companion. The woman and the girl have become quite good friends during Polly's stay at the house. She is polite, like so many country girls, and enjoys cleaning the house she dreams that she and her man will share one day.

Now she looks forward to a night with Doug by her side, sharing the excitement of a movie together, just the two of them.

They don't stay on the street for long because Doug is afraid of meeting an enraged, betrayed Pretty Boy or Silver and Polly is worried about seeing Jenny Campton or her mates. Both are afraid of the police. They go and sit in the elegant lounge of the cinema and smoke cigarettes until the picture starts.

It is a great movie, full of mystery and magic and intrigue. She curls up beside him on the seat and is content.

As they leave, Doug tells Polly to wait in the street while he goes to the toilet.

She leans back against the billboards of the various shows, still flushed with the night's pleasures. She lights up a cigarette and thinks happily of the night to come. They may go to a coffee bar or straight home. They may risk going to Gary's and play a game of pool. Then tomorrow, they will go to Peringrup and she will show him her country and her people and the places of her dreaming. She leans back and closes her eyes in languid reverie.

'Hullo, Polly. Having fun, are we?'

She opens her eyes, startled, and takes in the hard young face of the policewoman.

She springs from the wall and tries to run, but the woman's hand is grabbing her arm like a vice and she is hustled through the cheerful crowd leaving the theatre.

'Dougie! Dougie!' she cries, but everyone ignores her or stares at her curiously.

She is pushed into the back seat of the police car.

'I thought I recognised her,' the woman says triumphantly to her male companion. 'This one's been on the run for about three months now. And doing quite nicely for herself by the look of things.' She eyes Polly's dress, enviously.

They cruise away from the curb.

'Dougie,' Polly moans in anguish.

But he cannot hear. He is too busy making faces in the mirror, combing his hair and deciding on the hairstyle that suits him best. When at length he does emerge, he searches for Polly all over the cinema and along the street. He looks into Gary's and in to the coffee bar across from Gary's, where they have often gone. Only then does he realise what must have happened.

He feels miserable and utterly alone. Just half an hour ago they were side by side and her small hand was placed protectively on his knee. In the toned-down light of the cinema he glanced across at her sparkling eyes and flashing teeth.

Her tinkling laughter or hushed gasps are still fresh in his ear. He can still remember her perfume and her own particular smell.

Now the winds are colder and nothing matters any more. Not a single thing.

He sits on a form just down from where the Crystal Palace used to be and miserably lights a cigarette. He draws in the acrid smoke and lets it out slowly. Into his downcast vision swims a pair of heavy scuffed boots. Slowly he raises his eyes to see who the owner is; getting ready to run if it is Detective Maxwell.

It is Silver.

A Silver with a face as mean and as pale as Dracula's. He supports a giggling girl on his tattooed arm.

'My best mate, Doug,' he says coldly.

'G'day, Silver,' Doug returns nervously. 'What ya doin'?'

The youth necks with his companion and smiles faintly.

'What's it look like?' he says, sending his girl into fresh fits of giggling. Doug isn't sure that she's not stoned out of her head.

'Where's your old lady, Doug? Leave her at home, did you, while you eye over the local scenery?'

'No. Monaych caught 'er not half an hour ago.'

'Did they now? Isn't that a shame?' Silver grunts tonelessly and moves his dangerous boots closer. His eyes glare at the huddled, frightened Doug. 'It seems to me, Doug, everyone gets caught when they hang around you. Me, Polly, your daddy and cousin and uncle, Floyd too.'

'Unna?'

'I think that's really funny,' Silver carries on without the slightest amusement in his voice or his appearance.

'If ya tryin' to say I dobbed ya in, ya wrong!' Doug cries. 'Ask Polly — '

'I'd like to, Doug. But of course you didn't dob me in, pal. You and me are best mates, after all!' He turns to the girl, who isn't giggling so much now, but staring with wide-eyed wonder, realising that there may be a fight.

'Debbie, this is my best mate here, Dougo Dooligan, and we're just going to see another good mate, Pretty Boy Floyd. Aren't we, pal?' he says, menacingly.

'Pretty Boy's 'ere?' asks Doug nervously.

'They beat fuck out of him but he didn't admit to anything, so they had to let him go. He told them he bought this watch off a white bloke, but here's a funny thing,' and Silver bends close to a worried Doug, 'he gave you that watch, for a present like, so how does it happen they know *he* stole it? With all your brains, you can tell me that little thing, can you, Dougie?'

Silver effortlessly hauls Doug to his feet, and the three set off towards the Time Zone disco that stands where Crystals used to. Inside the front part is reserved for an impressive array of space age games. Pretty Boy's tall, lithe form crouches over one in which he is a rocket pilot killing all the space aliens who dive at him from everywhere, bombarding him mercilessly. He dodges and ducks and destroys, oblivious of all else, until he is finally blown up in a barrage of gunfire. He goes down fighting, though, taking two of the three remaining enemy with him.

'Shit,' he mutters, then spins around, grinning.

'Look at that, Silver, I skun you wicked,' he says, before seeing a guilty-looking Doug. His grin fades and he stares icily into Doug's face before beckoning him with a yellow finger to come outside.

Along the side of the building lurks an alley. Into this the two disappear while Silver keeps guard at the entrance.

'So what ya know, Dougie?'

'Listen, Pretty Boy, I never dobbed ya in,' Doug begins desperately, then cries out in alarm as knobbly fists push him back against the wall.

Pretty Boy pounces onto him and breathes ever so softly, 'Don't whine, ya whinging two-timin' cunt! I 'ate people 'oo can't face the facts of what they done. Them monaych, the Boys from Brazil, busted into Valerie's flat and they beat me up real

122

good, those pigs. They went and spoiled everything. What ya done, Doug, is done, and can't be undone.'

'Look, Pretty Boy, they beat me up, too. They even beat up Silver. Look, I didn't mean . . .'

Pretty Boy's hard fist slaps his head back into the wall. This hurts Doug even more because here is no bullying policeman but his best friend whom he has betrayed to the common enemy.

'Shut up before I pull you apart,' whispers Pretty Boy.

For a long moment the youths stare at each other. Behind Floyd's wildness there is confusion and bewilderment. He shakes his head and moves away from Doug's cringing figure.

'Aah, fuck it. What ya do it for, Dougie? Ya couldn't take an 'idin' like a man?'

Doug sniffs sadly.

'Aaaaah, shit — bugger everything. I can't 'it you, Dougie. I thought we was mates for life, but I dunno.'

He turns away. 'Go on away, Dougie. Just never let me see you again. We're finished.' Head down, he walks back to his game.

What does Doug walk away to? In one night he has lost his woman and his best and only friend. He feels as though both crutches have been kicked from under his armpits and all the gods are closing in to boot him to a smashed-up nullity.

For the rest of that week Doug works listlessly at the stables, his heart no longer in his work.

When he came back the night Polly was taken he asked his mother for help for the first time in his life. She rang up the home and tried to find out why Polly was being held; she said she would gladly look after her if she was released into her custody. But they said it would take time and they were not altogether happy because Polly would probably just go back on the streets, stealing again.

So now Doug walks a lonely path beside the cold gloomy river where he and Polly have had such happy times. He will lie for hours, it seems, and stare blankly into the grey, morbid skies. He will lie sleepless in his bed, empty except for the ache in his heart.

On the Friday morning, as he busies himself tidying up the

stalls and heaving bags of grain into storage, he hears subdued voices. He peeps over the stall gate to see the Boys from Brazil clustered around Mr Foley, who, even as he looks, points in Doug's dismayed direction.

This is it. Amidst all the rustling hay and secretive rats and mice, with the air full of grain smells and horse sweat and molasses and horseshit smells, he will be siezed and taken to the glass dungeons of the CIB castle.

The three men squelch through the yellowish water and dodge the sweet-odoured green-brown mounds. Doug pretends to ignore them and sweeps furiously until a gentle voice says, 'Well, you're a working man now, Doug. That's very good indeed.'

He turns to face them, trying to feel safe in his environment. They cannot hurt him here, he tells himself wildly. This is not their world. Nor is it truly his world, but he is getting used to it and he loves it. The Boys from Brazil only understand a shady dark criminal world, with all its troubles and its stuffy office work. They look out of place here in their suits and shiny shoes.

'Bad luck about your Dad, wasn't it, Doug?' the small, sinister man says. 'What do you know about that?'

'Nothin',' Doug sulks.

'The one who got away, well, we know who he is,' the big driver rumbles, eyes piercing into Doug's.

Doug doesn't flinch or flicker one bit, just stares coldly back so the driver is reminded of Carey Dooligan's calm stare.

'So why don't ya go and catch 'im, instead of talkin' to honest labourers?' he says.

'We like to check up on you, Doug. Make sure you're not stealing things from your employer.'

'Ya told Mr Foley that, I s'pose. That'd just make ya fuckin' day,' Doug snarls, becoming angry.

'Careful, Doug. We can take you down to Central any day we choose. You're on the danger list now in our books,' the infuriatingly quiet man says.

He moves close to the skinny youth. 'The thing is, Dougie, you're not clever enough to get anywhere or be anything big.

You're just stupid enough to always be the one caught,' he smiles.

'Well, guess what?' Doug smiles back, 'ya never caught me yet.'

'But we will!' the man replies. 'We will, Dougie, old son. Then you'll wish you'd never been born, my old bucket of snail-shit.' His fingers reach out and he mildly pinches Doug's cheek. 'Be good, Dougie,' he murmurs.

They drift away and out of the yard, while Doug watches them leave with a faraway look in his deadened eyes. Mr Foley watches Doug.

At the end of his half day's work, Mr Foley pays his week's wages. As Doug starts to walk away, he calls out, 'We won't need you now, Doug. The yards are all fixed and the stables tidy enough. Thanks.'

'But, Mr Foley, I thought I might work here for longer. There's lots to do, really,' says Doug.

'No, there's no more work,' the old man says with finality.

Doug fingers his last pay cheque and stares at the old man, with sad, knowing eyes.

His mother, making him a lunchtime coffee to warm him up after work, sees he is depressed and hugs him to her.

'What's the matter, dear? Still worrying 'bout Polly? We'll go and visit her on the weekend if you like.'

'No, it's not Polly. It's everything,' he sighs, then he sits down and tells her all about the other night, with Hughie and his Dad.

She is shocked but not surprised. In fact, when she read the paper's account and saw Polly's eyes, she had a feeling the missing thief was her son. She touches him soothingly on the shoulder.

'Well then, darling, there is just one thing you can do and that is to go and stay with Jemima. As a matter of fact, Jamie was talking about getting an extra hand — there are several jobs to do around the place.'

'Now, Mum, ya know me and Jamie don't get on. 'E'll break my bones, so 'e will.'

'Don't be ridiculous,' she snaps.

'I wish I was like Tom. 'E was real brainy, ya know. Still, 'ard work'll get me strong again, I s'pose,' he says thoughtfully and gives a half smile. 'Plenty of that with Jamie around. Build up me muscles.'

She stares at him for a long time. It is not often they discuss Tom. At last she says softly, 'You don't need muscles to get somewhere in life, Doug. You must just be yourself and know yourself. Now, I'll ring Jemima and tell her you're coming down, if Jamie can pick you up. Don't let's have this nonsense about Jamie hating you. He's a good boy; and besides, Willie is there and the new baby. Anyway, you always liked the country. And I'm not having you sit around here idle, waiting for the police to pick you up.'

That afternoon in the parole office, Doug has some good news for Mr Salvadorez.

Jamie arrives next morning in a decrepit grey utility with old straw and an old black-and-white Border Collie in the back.

Jamie McDonald is thirty years old, a contented and self-satisfied man in the prime of his life. He has a fine wife and two equally fine children and a fine tract of land. Everything in his life is fine — except for his snivelling, undernourished and sneaky brother-in-law.

Jamie doesn't tolerate weakness in anyone, for he has never been weak. He has a good business mind and, once he starts something, he won't stop until it's done and done perfectly. That is why his farm is so well run and why neither he nor his family wants for anything.

He has always awed Doug because of his muscular frame just a few centimetres less than two metres tall and his shrewd, scornful eyes that look into Doug and read all his mistakes and misfortunes.

Jamie is courtesy itself when he is with Edith, his mother-in-law. He stands by while Doug lets her kiss and hug him goodbye, then they are away, Doug waving and Jamie blowing the wheezy old horn.

126

They are hardly around the corner when Jamie's emerald green eyes turn on Doug.

'Let's get one thing straight, Doug. I'm letting you work on the farm for a hundred bucks a week; that's fifty more than you're getting on the dole. But if you try using me up, like you use your Mum, I'll kick you so hard in the arse you'll end up in bloody Albany. Do we understand each other?'

Doug stares sullenly out the window.

'Yes,' the giant smiles, 'looks like we understand each other perfectly.'

There is not much traffic at this hour on a Saturday morning and, as the houses thin out and the road becomes lined with orchards or market gardens, what traffic there is disappears. Doug is glad to be leaving the city, with its row upon rows of houses and buildings forming a turbulent grey sea, a place where fish ate fish and there is no mercy at all.

The two don't talk much. Jamie dislikes Doug as much as Doug dislikes police. The youth hates Jamie for being what he is; one of the tin dummies who inadvertently killed his brother. For Tom and his strange friends looked into life and found the great love there, whereas the tin men march through life without even looking at it. They are born, they die and they think they have had a good life. Tom, who sat and squeezed every delectable drop he could get from his short gentle existence, frightened them. It seems unfair that Jamie and countless others like him should live on, keeping the world as it is, while the poet and philosopher Tommy Dooligan is mouldering in some unmarked grave.

They pull up at the Halfway House, a well-established cafe and service station. Once it was used as a stopover for the stagecoach that ran south, since it is roughly halfway between Perth and Williams, the next biggest town. Ruling the roads then, it rules them now.

Doug and Jamie buy a steak each and wolf into the food, gulping down cups of hot black tea. Between gulps, slurps and burps, Jamie explains to Doug the work he will do: mostly clearing and fencing, since the seeding has been done and the shearing is yet to start. This is the time of year for burning off, sucker bashing and odd jobs around the farmyard.

Doug listens with half an ear, concentrating on his food and the chatter of the girls behind the counter. Because he feels so happy and free, he gives one of them a cheeky wink, and when she returns it, he looks at her again.

She has chestnut hair and a sly lipsticked smile. Her frank blue eyes challenge him.

'Can I get a can of Coke, Jamie?'

'Yeah, just don't stick up the place, kid.'

'I couldn't stick nothin' up your place, mate, since ya already got ya own finger jammed right there,' Doug mocks, cutting Jamie's laugh short.

He buys a can, sensing the girl leaning on the counter, appraising his thin body. He mutters so only she can hear, 'See ya sometime, honey. I only live just down the track.'

'What makes you think I want to see you?' she grins.

'Because I'm too guritch, look. Mr Perth, I am.'

'Well, big boy, don't get lost in your coat.' She giggles at the frail body enveloped in the heavy greatcoat he has bought himself.

He clicks his tongue and winks, sending her into fresh giggles

She is about eighteen and quite nice-looking; a little bit fat, but what does that matter?

He swaggers back to Jamie, grinning hugely. Jamie scowls, still smarting from Doug's last remark.

'What's so funny, you dopey bastard?'

'Everything funny about you, anyways,' retorts Doug.

'I'm going to beat your head in before long, you silly bastard,' Jamie states matter-of-factly and gets up.

They drive on through the awakening day, passing clusters of trees and sheep and cattle. Everywhere the undulating land is fresh and green and Doug sniffs in the sweet, lush nectar.

They pass Tunneyville, where the extensive Tunney family once lived all together, each son building his own house, so there were about four houses clustered around the highway. Doug's

Mum used to tell him that the Tunneys were the only people in the district to have a telephone and how everyone used to come and ring up, so the Tunneys' place was the social centre of the district in those days. There were four generations of Tunneys; that is what a dynasty means, Doug supposes. The Tunneys are quite unlike the Dooligan clan who are scattered all over Australia, wherever the Dooligan brothers' whims and wanderings took them, or like the Menzies, who had no sons. Now the Tunneys also have no sons and their mansions are decaying into memories.

Just past Tunneyville, Jamie turns onto the Wandaring road. They are nearly home: Doug will soon be with his sister, his nephew, his new little niece and all the peace he needs.

Doug surprises Jamie by muttering softly.

'Thanks, Jamie, for givin' me this job. Ya one good bloke sometimes.'

'Just sometimes?' the giant answers, dodging potholes on the track leading to the house. But he is pleased.

Doug smiles quietly.

All along the roadside scruffy, ravaged pines, with their dark-green foliage etched against the sky, peer down at Doug and breathe a soft song of homecoming to him. He glances around at all the old familiar buildings clinging to the hill and is content.

The car stops amidst frenzied barking from the several tied-up Kelpies and Border Collies. A weak sun gleams down from its cloudy domain.

The house is about fifty years old, having been built by old Iain McDonald, Jamie's father. It is not a large house, since the old McDonalds had only one child. Doug is to sleep in the shearers' quarters, which suits him because he likes being alone.

He drops his battered brown case on the bed that Jemima has made for him and smiles at the vase of bright flowers picked for him and standing on the cracked, dusty dresser. Then he strolls outside and into the house.

This house truly is a home, with baby things strewn around and the warmth of flames and love drifting everywhere. It has pictures and posters on the wall. A young house, this one, clasping its occupants close to its weatherboard heart.

Jemima sits sewing by the fire while the baby sleeps and the little boy plays.

What a reunion it is, with Willie's childish babblings at the sight of the uncle he hasn't seen for two years. That and Jemima's smile, like the rising dawn, are the best things Doug has seen for quite a while.

Jemima has the darkest red hair of all the Dooligan children, but she does not have the temper that redheads are reputed to have. She is frail and gentle, quiet and calm, strength is hidden behind her wide blue eyes and large, sensuous mouth.

She loves everyone, even her wild rough young brother whom she cannot understand. She and Doug talk about old times (delicately skirting the subject of jail) and relax in front of the fire.

Afterwards Jamie takes Doug for a bumpy ride around the farm, showing him the fences that need fixing and the paddocks that need clearing.

'You can have this ute, Doug. It's getting a bit rickety, but it'll do. So you can be your own boss and work your own way, the way you liked to before.'

Back in the sheds he is shown where to find all the equipment he needs. Then they go back inside.

'Too bloody cold to work, Doug, and I never get my workmen to do things *I* wouldn't do. We'll have a charge of rum,' says Jamie, in one of his rare affable moods.

For the rest of that afternoon, the men have a peaceful drink and play a game of chess that becomes increasingly complicated the more rum they drink. They laugh at each other's mistakes and Doug's cautious face often expresses a gaiety that he has been missing these last two years. He feels part of the family once again.

That night the rain tattooing upon the tin walls and roof of the hut and the trickling as it runs down into the mud of the yard lull him into a soothing sleep.

The next morning, as the sun stretches over the treetops and heavy clouds float up from the south, he sneaks into the kitchen and grabs some bread, then sets off to fix up the fences.

This country is his Shangri-La, where all things are eternally young and bountiful and beauty is everywhere. There is no such thing as ugliness, since even ugliness is beautiful here. Every morning he disappears over the hills and into the bush, with Tess, the old black-and-white Border Collie, beside him for company. He rejoices in his work of tightening the twisted wire fences, sometimes having to thread in new wire and once or twice sinking a new post. So his tune is the thudding of the axe or the creaking of the wire, gasps and occasional swear words and the clatter of his tools.

The cool, tangy air washes the red from his eyes and the drink from his brain. He becomes sharp-eyed and alert and happy, as he was on his father's farm. Often he will rest, with the dog beside him, and smoke a relaxing cigarette while he listens to the sounds of his bush and the silence all around him.

There is the murmuring of the trees and the muttering of the rain, the raucous shouts of the black cockatoos and the chattering of the smaller birds, the whistles of the parrots in their cavalier dress, bright and flashy. Then, of course, there are the warbling magpies whose call is as melodious as their feathers are dull. Kookaburras' cruel, maniacal laughter from the hills some distance away, warns the smaller birds to beware of these squat, jolly butchers.

Doug marvels at Nature, pure and simple.

Sometimes rain whips at the quivering trees and the air is filled with thunder as the great black clouds rear and prance like Pluto's horses. Then Doug curls up in the cab with the old dog and watches the magnificent fury of the storm. The rain lashes at the windows and the wind shakes the ute in an icy rage, but it is all to no avail. Doug reads comics until the sky's fury is spent.

He feels very close to the wild, just as his dusky ancestors did, huddled together in their gunyahs; just as his Celtic ancestors would have stood upon the clifftops of angry Arran, hearing the thunderous cry of the sea and feeling a surge through their hearts.

Doug starts putting up a new fence, cutting a paddock in two. He rigs up a tarpaulin over the back of the ute and packs a box with provisions, then camps out for a fortnight, seeing no-one at all, for this is an isolated part of the property. When he feels bored, he listens to his radio and learns several songs off by heart.

At night, by the smoking fire, he thinks mostly of Polly and sometimes of his mother and Pretty Boy. But always Polly's face flickers and takes shape among the elusive flames. That is the only time he feels lonely.

He grunts and sweats and digs the long line of holes that appear as red-brown earth or orange-pink clay mounds upon the virginal green hill. Then he drives in and loads up the posts he can carry. Jamie offers to help him but Doug replies, 'No, Jamie. This is goin' to be my fence, what *I* built and no-one else. I want something to show that I was 'ere and done some good. A monument, sort of, ya know?'

Jamie stares at him and wonders if perhaps jail has changed his sly, untrustworthy brother-in-law into someone he can be more or less proud of. He seems to be quieter, not drunk all the time. And he *is* working, thinks Jamie.

So the posts start to go up, slowly and painstakingly. Their silhouette jags into the white cotton wool clouds as they crawl over the hill and it gives Doug a sense of achievement every time he brings more posts.

One afternoon Jamie comes out and asks him if he would like to go the Wandaring pub, since it is Friday, after all. Doug has been saving his money as there is little to spend it on down here except cigarettes. He draws some from his tin box and the two men set off. Jemima and the kids stay home, not terribly impressed by the rowdiness of the local hotel.

It is crowded with damp jostling figures trying to get warm on a cold Friday night. They play pool and darts and talk and joke: it is interesting talk about local identities and coming attractions. If he was in Perth, Doug thinks, he would be loitering around the streets now. Since he has been down here he has begun to see what a wasted life *that* was.

In the corner some Aboriginals sit. Doug recognizes two of the Dawson boys, one of whom he has met several times with Floyd. They acknowledge his smile with slight nods, then their eyes, as dark as the swirling night, disappear into their own thoughts and their own world. Doug moves off to play pool with his booming brother-in-law.

Later, they sing and swerve their way home, drunk as lords. They stumble in their own directions, to their own bed and dreams.

He dreams of Polly. He dreams of the fence he is making — a part of him — stretched over the gentle hill he loves so.

Yet he never does finish the fence.

Love will waft through your veins and poison you with sweet slow rhythm, but trouble, when it comes, is as fast and dangerous as a striking taipan.

10

There comes a day when the rain is so heavy that Doug cannot risk driving the old ute over the quagmire of mud and the treacherous slippery grass and clay. So he stays around cleaning up the sheds, making salt licks and storing all the bags of grain so they don't get wet.

He is having a well-earned rest and rolling a smoke when the dogs start barking and he hears, over the subdued roar of the rain, the muffled groaning of a motor car churning up the muddy track between the buildings. He doesn't care if it is Jamie, who has lapsed into his brusque mood and who will tell him off for being slack. He is just so buggered. He had forgotten how heavy superphosphate is and how the powder stings every sore on his hands.

But it is not Jamie. It is Pretty Boy.

He is resplendent in skin-tight jeans and cowboy boots and a bright red silk shirt. Behind him straggle Silver and Shagger.

Doug, remembering when they last parted, feels apprehensive and tries to remember where the bale hook is in case Silver comes for him, or even Pretty Boy.

But the Aboriginal youth's lopsided grin and cheerful eyes reassure him. For, in truth, Floyd Davey has really missed Doug. He has forgotten and forgiven all Doug's shortcomings. He has missed Doug's jokes and his money and he feels sorry for hitting Doug after he learned that his woman had been taken.

'G'day, Dougie, ya black bastard,' he cries and jumps upon him, lifting him up and throwing him onto the bags. They both wrestle and laugh for a moment, then they sit up.

'Yeah, Dougie,' Silver grins. 'Surprised to see us turn up, I'll bet. Turn up like a bad smell, we do.'

Doug remembers the Dawsons in the pub and understands how they have found him.

'We're workin' on Danny Jacobs' farm now, just across from 'ere,' Floyd says. 'Cruel good bloke, old Danny is. 'E lets us go at any ol' time. We come to see if ya goin' to the pub now.'

'I gotta work,' says Doug.

'That's what the sheila said, too, down at the house, but you're not doing much of that, Dougie, lyin' around on your butt,' Shagger smiles.

'Well, wait 'ere, youse blokes,' Doug says and goes to the far end of the sea of bags. He ducks his slim hand down and emerges with an almost full flagon of sweet muscat.

'Fuck me, Dougo, you believe in the good life,' Silver whoops.

'Not much work going' on 'ere, orright, drinkin' gabba and smokin'. Where's all the yorgas?' Pretty Boy grins.

Doug, feeling happy with his friends and glad to be accepted again, disappears into one of the sheepyards. He emerges a few moments later transformed into a woman of sorts, with the help of some sheep's wool, an old bag and two tins. He minces over to the grinning youths and man.

'Am, excuse me, am, my name is Nora Tittoff and I just really think ya the most lovely things I never did see.'

'Can I take ya 'ome with me? I reckon ya solid,' grins Pretty Boy, then he stands and bows. 'Can I have this dance?'

'Oh, I only just met you. Do you think we should?' Nora Tittoff answers coyly.

Doug and Pretty Boy waltz around the shed with ungainly steps, as do Silver and Shagger, joining in the fun. They collapse in helpless joy and wipe the tears of laughter from their faces.

'Oh, you're a funny bloke, Dougie,' Floyd sighs.

So they drink some of the flagon, and Pretty Boy tells Doug the news from Perth. The same old things: fights, girls and crimes. Football. At the last football match all the Nyler boys, up from Albany, finally caught up with Pretty Boy. They cornered him and one of the Palmer boys as they left the grounds and there was a fight. Floyd still carries a bottle scar across his flat black chest. The police have started coming around because he has a fine to pay, so they decided to go bush for a while and here they are.

They hide the flagon away for a future date, then they troop out to Shagger's grand panel van, sulking amongst the farmyard mess and dribbling in the rain. Doug, feeling drunk and sick of the heavy superphosphate anyway, is persuaded to join them. Shagger guns the engine and sprays mud everywhere, then they skid around to the shearers' quarters, where Doug rushes in to get some money. They do snakeys all over the road on their way out and Doug falls back laughing into the dubious way of life from the past.

They drink and play pool or darts all afternoon, in the near-deserted pub, and they get drunk. At early nightfall they drive Doug home, all brothers and friends and happy together.

Jamie is in a bad mood; if Doug was sober he would realise this. But he is in a dozy stupor from too much drink and fun. He slumps at the table and chews his food slowly, with a quiet smile playing about his lips.

'Where were you this afternoon?' Jamie bursts out.

'In the pub, drinkin'.'

'Who with?'

'No-one special.' Doug puts his fork down and stares into his brother-in-law's angry eyes.

'I know who it was,' says Jamie.

'Well, what ya askin' me for then?' Doug snarls, feeling tipsy and brave and tired of Jamie's moods.

'I pay you to work on this farm, not to piss off and get drunk with those louts, the cheap little bastards. Besides, I don't want any boongs on the place.'

'Well, my own Dad's a boong, so you'd better get used to boongs on the place,' Doug sneers. 'Your kid's great-grandmother is a true blue 'alf-caste, Jamie. What ya think of that?'

He has touched the one flaw in Jamie's fine world. At night sometimes, the man cannot help thinking that beside him in the bed, is a woman whose ancestors are Aboriginal. For all Jemima's beauty and kindness, this gives him a strange feeling.

Now he bounds up from the table and comes towards Doug, crying, 'You shut your dirty mouth.'

Before Doug knows what he is doing, he is up out of his chair and brandishing the gravy-stained carving knife.

Jamie stops. For a long moment they stare at each other, then Jamie sits down again, as does Doug.

'You gutless wonder,' Jamie says slowly. 'I reckon you would have gone for me too, wouldn't you?'

Just then Jemima comes in from the living-room at the other end of the house.

'What on earth are you two shouting about?' she asks.

Both men chew their roast beef and avoid her eyes.

'Well, I must say you've certainly gone quiet now.'

' 'E was just practisin' for the football.' Dougie points his fork at Jamie.

'When you finish, you boys, come and keep me company.'

Then she swishes out and the eyes of the two men lock again like dogs arguing over a bone.

'If you ever try that stunt again, I'll tear you into mouseshit,' says Jamie. 'Do you understand?'

Doug nods, afraid not of Jamie but of himself. He knows that if the giant had come any closer he would have stabbed him. Once blood is sighted, he thinks, he will keep on drawing blood like a killer dog, until the howling hunters ride him down.

'You'd better understand, shithead. Now get out there and keep your sister company.'

Doug goes to bed early that night and dreams that he really does stab Jamie. As the man dies he turns into Jemima, so Doug wakes up, sweating. He rolls and smokes a cigarette and wishes Polly was beside him. Out camping, the bush was his mistress and he held it to him as closely as any woman. But now he wants

Polly's dusky loins around him and her soft voice comforting him and her large, brown eyes swamping him and driving away all his fears.

Early in the morning he is awoken by Jemima.

'Dougie, we forget to tell you last night, but we're going down to Albany for a party, so you'll be here all day by yourself. Jamie was wondering if you could clean out underneath the sheep pens: Goodbye, darling,' she kisses his still sleepy face and goes out, turning at the door. 'Oh, and lunch is in the fridge, in the alfoil, but we should be back by teatime.'

Trust Jamie to give him a shitty job when the big bastard is in a shitty mood, thinks Doug. The underneath of the shed is knee-deep in dried sheep droppings and rats and countless spiders may be found there. Besides, he will have to crawl, since it is too low to stand.

Doug moans and turns over to sleep, since he has had a restless night. Things are starting to go sour now, he thinks.

He has been happy here on his own; perhaps he should pick himself up and wander away from this life. Go over east, or up north, where no-one knows him and he can start all over again, just as he told himself he would, night after night, in the prison. The nights were the worst times, he remembers.

Prison is like his shadow and he drags it after him wherever he goes. Sometimes it almost disappears and at other times it stretches long and alive in front of or behind him. It never disappears completely and it never will for as long as he lives.

But he cannot go yet. Up in Perth, a fat, oily, well-meaning man has control of him, like a voodoo witch doctor, and he is a wax doll. Locked away in the unemotional grey cabinet, as effectively as he was behind iron bars, is his file. A piece of him, all in black and white.

He groans and mutters and rolls out of bed. He has a lingering hot shower which makes him feel better.

He dawdles around the yards, feeding up and collecting the eggs from the stupid-eyed hens. He plays with Tess before the old dog roams away on some journey of her own. Then he goes into the house for a cup of tea.

While he waits for the cheerful kettle to boil, his restless gaze falls upon Jamie's keys to his new Rover.

The Rover itself sits out in the garage, like one of Jamie's stud bulls. It represents achievement; a sign of equality, even superiority, for Jamie McDonald has finally made it and can move amongst his peers with self-esteem. The McDonalds have always been regarded by the older established gentry as being slightly lower on the social scale. Besides, old Iain has often rubbed people up the wrong way with his Highlander bluntness. But now his son has gone to a public school and built the property into something worthwhile. He has a gorgeous wife and two nice children and a brand new Rover, low and silver and shining.

Doug's wily eyes gaze at those keys now, as though he is in a trance: like a bird before a darting, dancing cobra.

If he borrowed the car, just think what a figure he would cut, he ponders. He would be back before Jamie arrives home and — why not? — he could pick up that piece at the Halfway House. They would take a spin up to Perth and he could ride around the streets like a knight on his silver charger, or a sly robber with his Maid Marian beside him. He remembers what Pretty boy told him once: 'If ya got a car, buddy, you can pick up any yorga. Girls like a boy with a car. Ya king of the world!'

As he rolls a smoke and listens to the kettle whistling in the cold, lonely kitchen, the idea seems better every minute.

It is good to sit behind the wheel of the glossy, sensuous car. It gives him a sense of power he has never had before. He drives carefully at first, then, as his hands become used to the movements of his new machine, he puts on speed and revels in its power.

He arrives at the Halfway House at mid-morning. He parks the car in a glorious skid at the front of the restaurant and bounds up the steps. He pauses to talk to the moulting, sulking galah in the smelly cage, who stares back wordlessly with black eyes.

'Useless bloody bird. I'll eat ya,' he whispers fiercely in good humour, and chuckles as the bird waddles away on its perch.

In the restaurant he sees the girl cleaning up the tables. He props himself against the ice-cream container and studies her lascivious body as he has watched Silver and Pretty Boy do to many a slack girl.

She turns and spots him, recognising him in that foolish great-coat he insists on wearing, the one that seems twice too big for his slender form. Surprise flashes across her eyes and an impish smile spreads across her face. She moves up to him, very much aware of his eyes on her tight, provocative dress.

Her perfume drifts into his nose and brain.

'Well, hullo, champ! Where'd you spring from?'

'Oh, I bin places. I'd of been 'ere earlier, but I'ad important business in Sydney,' he grins.

'What, pickin' up the rubbish?' She smiles back and stands in the position that shows off her body to its best advantage. 'So what are you doin'?'

'Nothin' special,' he says as he takes a bottle of Coke from the fridge. 'Got this on the house, eh, honey?'

'You've got a nerve,' she teases, and puts her hands on her hips, emphasising her bosom. 'How do you know I'm not married?'

He takes a swig of his Coke. He knows that what he has sensed about her the first time is right; she will go with anyone if he has the money. A quick hello, a bit of fun, then a clean goodbye; it's quick and clean love that can be used over and over again with no worries.

'I'll tell ya why ya not married. ''Cos the only ring that Diana's got is the ring around her — '' 'he winks and drinks again while she titters.

She likes him, with his roan hair all awry and the hint of strength in his bony body, with his haunting eyes and ghost of a smile.

'My name isn't Diana, it's Angelina,' she says.

'Well, mine's Doug. Ya know what?' he smirks, and leans close to her. 'Angelina's such a nice name I want ya to come for a ride to Perth with me: I got monies 'cos I just got paid, but I got

140

no-one to spend it on.'

'OK, big boy. I'll tell the boss. You go and wait outside.'

He wanders out and leans against the side of the Rover.

'We're right for the day,' he whispers to the gleaming car, and pushes Polly from his mind. Angelina hurries out, with a flushed look about her face and her eyes sparkling with adventure.

''Ow'd ya get out?'

'Oh, I just said Mum was sick and my brother had come to pick me up,' she states, sliding into the front seat and making sure she shows a lot of stockinged leg. Oh, wow! he whistles to himself, she knows all the tricks. He thinks back to his years before jail with Floyd and Silver and all the girls they used to grab, like this one here. The other two did all the grabbing, really; he just watched, not knowing the vocabulary that would turn the key to their vixen hearts. He thinks briefly and guiltily of Polly again, but she is on the inside looking out, and he is on the outside looking in. They never seem to make it to life's great gift, whatever it is.

'This your car, champ?' she says, noticeably impressed.

'Yeah. Course, I'd a brought the Rolls Royce if I'd a known I was meetin' you,' he replies, then puts the accelerator down and they fishtail out onto the highway.

She starts right away, cuddling up to his sinewy form and laying her chestnut head in the crook of his neck. Experienced fingers crawl and explore him. He wraps an arm around her, claiming her for the while.

He feels like Shagger, with a new woman and a new car and lots of new notes in his pocket. For one day he can be someone. And the stories he will tell his mates tomorrow will make Pretty Boy's fights sound like fairy tales.

They talk about each other for a while, but mostly of what they'll spend Doug's money on. They discover they both know Arley Dawson and Murray Reeds, so laugh about them and their adventures.

They reach Perth an hour later, happy enough in each other's company.

Perth. The bush, with its gentle feathery fingers, has brushed away his thoughts about the city. Yet here it stands, grey and shadowed amid the dull coldness of drizzling rain, like a cobweb. Vehicles buzz like flies, and people run through the wet atmosphere. The Rover slows to a crawl and loses itself in the great, heaving mass.

They go to the afternoon session of the movies, seeing a war film that they don't have to concentrate on too much; they can attend to their own interests. Afterwards they wander hand in hand around the gloomy streets, window shopping. They go to an elegant coffee lounge, where the waitress is a little dubious of Doug's style of dress and the faint farm odours still clinging to him; after one look at his hard young face she doesn't say anything.

'Must be a change to be served instead of servin', unna?' He smiles across at Angelina.

'Sure is,' she smiles back. He has done what was expected of him and now it is her move.

'Let's go for a ride after,' she murmurs, catching his brown hand in her own manicured white ones.

'Why not? Buy a charge first, though. 'Ave our own party, what ya reckon?' he breathes back, all bravado gone now that the moment has arrived.

They pull in at a bottle shop, on the way out of the city and Doug buys two bottles of Jim Beam and a bottle of Coke.

'Celebrate with somethin' special.'

'What are you celebratin'? The loss of your virginity?' she giggles, not knowing how close to the truth she really is.

'Nuh, 'oo ya see 'ere is the biggest bull in the paddock,' he boasts.

'Moooo,' she bellows and they explode into laughter so that he almost runs the car off the road in mirth.

They slide out of the oily, clustered, crowded city and are back into the State forest. As though it is glad to be away from all its snuffling brethren, the Rover erupts into powerful joy, fishtailing all over the road and leaving black skid marks on the grey bends just as a dog pisses on a post to show that it has claimed its territory.

Angelina opens one of the whisky bottles and finds a plastic cup in the glove compartment. She fills it half with Coke and half with whisky and shares it with Doug.

They soon come to a shaggy track almost hidden by stunted bushes. A yellow sign proclaims that everyone is to beware of logging trucks crossing, as well as to keep out.

There will be no logging trucks at this hour and in this weather. They nose up into the wild brush and presently find themselves in an orderly plantation of young pine trees. He stops the car and there is only the breathing of the girl and the sighing from the darkening sky. The whispering of the rain and the trees tell him to go home and leave this girl with the eyes of Lethe, but Doug, drinking more of the mellow yellow elixir, falls into his damn-everybody rut and has eyes only for her.

He becomes drunk enough to fall onto her and peel away her clothes, muttering meaningless endearments. Naked, they struggle into the back seat, giggling from the whisky and the difficulties encountered. On the plush sheepskin covers, he reaps the reward that his money and patience sowed and grew. They love and drink and love and sleep; at least, they make what they think is love.

The stars above stare down, as beautiful as Andromeda and as faithful as Moera, while soft fingers of rain tap on the car windows and night peeps anxiously in to remind the fuddled youth of his duties. But it is too late; Doug sleeps in the pale, purple-nailed hands of his witchy woman.

He wakens in the early greyness of morning. They have made a nest of their clothes and he feels warm from the sleeping girl beside him and lazy from last night's whisky.

His position dawns on him almost immediately, with shocking clarity.

Morning! God love me, Jamie'll be ropable with his car gone! Doug panics. Shit, what a way to go.

He springs from the back, waking the girl, who stretches sleepily.

'Quick,' he cries, 'we gotta get dressed!'

She doesn't seem so pretty now, with her tousled hair and her sleep-bleared eyes and her makeup all smudged away. They dress hurriedly and the girl cannot suppress a giggle at the sight of the frantic Doug hopping around the small clearing, half in and half out of his trousers.

'Jesus, I'm a dead man,' he mumbles as they get into the car. He doesn't even bother to put on his coat or boots.

She cuddles up close to him, trying to catch some of yesterday, but yesterday is as far away as the disappearing night in the western sky.

'No, bugger ya! I gotta concentrate,' he snaps, afraid, and pushes her away. She moves over to her side of the car and looks outside, her eyes as glassy as the window. She's been finished with.

He guns the motor and wrenches the Rover savagely along the highway, until they reach the Halfway House, just down the way a little.

'See ya, Angie. And thanks, ya know,' he says in the old mood, realising that all else is lost and trying to catch some of last night's enjoyment.

But she is still sulking and slams the door in his face. He won't see her again.

He spins viciously out of the yard, sending up mud and stones and bringing a curse from the proprietor, who is swabbing the verandah and conversing with the galah.

'Look at him, the bloody young twit. I can't see what she sees in them, meself. Brother, indeed,' he scoffs, 'that one has a different brother every week.'

The galah agrees, yelling rowdily like the larrikin it is.

Maybe they haven't come back yet, thinks Doug. If the party went all night, they won't be home. The car might have broken down. Anything could have happened.

But he knows it is hopeless.

He passes the police van just past Tunneyville. It swerves around after him, its siren sounding eerily in the morning mists.

He feels as a fox must feel, backed up in a shallow cave with the baying triumphant hounds and the pealing of the gentleman hunter's horn the last sound in his ears.

He doesn't run, though; there is no point. He slows down and pulls to the side of the road.

He watches the van pull in front of him, watches the two men get out, the driver nodding to the other when he reads the number plates. He follows the two men's journey towards him, with lacklustre eyes.

'Oh, shit,' he mutters. One policeman is peering in at him.

'Your name Douglas Dooligan?'

'Yeah,' he says in a flat, dead voice.

'You got a licence?'

'Nuh,' in the same dead tone.

'Get out, will you, son?'

Doug obeys slowly, wondering what will happen to him on this lonely stretch of road that only yesterday beckoned him on, inviting and wicked.

When he stands up, the questioner towers over him like a karri or a mountain. All Doug's dreams have vanished like the night's fogs that it drags behind as it scurries over the trees and hills. They have left Doug defenceless before the gimlet eyes, as grey as his own: as bright as the new day.

'Well, son, I suppose you know what you did?'

Doug remains downcast and silent, his bare feet digging nervously into the gravelly roadside and the winds of centuries tearing into his shaking, coatless body.

'Your sister and brother-in-law are scared to death and your Mum is nearly dead with worry,' the man rumbles. 'Half the district is out looking for you, wasting their time. On the properties, along the roads, at the Halfway House.'

Doug stiffens and risks a look at the Sergeant's stony, impassive face. Hard eyes dig into his soul before he drops his gaze.

'All the while, you were living it up with a cheap tart in town,' the man continues. 'Well, as long as you have a good time, bugger the rest, eh, son?'

For all his size, the Sergeant is a gentle man, yet he seems to have difficulty keeping his temper with this mute delinquent. If only Doug would try to defend himself, the man could hit back with words. As it is, his fists clench by his side in frustrated anger at all the trouble this uncaring youth has caused.

'If I were your brother-in-law, I'd know what to do with *you*.'

Doug stares up, with fire behind his eyes for just a second, daring him to try. Then he shuffles his feet, coughs throatily and looks away.

He is like a wild thing, trapped and knowing he is going to die. He has slipped into apathy.

The constable, who has spent the entire session staring at Doug, with emotionless eyes full of contempt, butts in, 'I'll ring up and tell them the kid's been found, Sarge.'

'Yeah, Andy. You drive the Rover and I'll take care of the kid,' the Sergeant grunts, then pushes Doug over to the front seat of the cold, cheerless van. No sheepskin covers or heaters or radios here; just an old weary sergeant who chastises a dead-hearted Doug all the way to the farm.

'Why'd you do it, Doug? You a bit simple, or something, that you should hurt your own family? Gawd, you get one every day, don't you, but: smart little pricks, who think they know it all. Tell me about this sheila you banged, Doug. Was she worth all the shit you're in now, kiddo?'

Merciless words, tearing up his day of glory. Yet it was nothing like glory really. She was neither Cleopatra nor Venus, just a painted woman looking for some games, as he was. When he is rotting in prison for the deeds he has done this day, she won't care a cent. She won't visit him; not like Polly Yarrup. He feels sick at his betrayal of the imprisoned girl, who truly is his Queen of Sheba.

This is how he arrives at the McDonalds', with a glowering, scoffing police escort and the cause of all his troubles chugging tamely behind.

The police don't wait around. They warn Doug that he may appear in court for driving without a licence; whether the charge of unlawful use of a motor vehicle will be brought against him depends on Jamie, and Jamie doesn't look very happy.

Doug and his brother-in-law are left alone in the kitchen, while Jemima stays with the children, out of the way.

'Are you going to apologise?' Jamie asks coldly.

'Well, sorry,' Doug mumbles.

'Let's hear it again, as though you really mean it,' Jamie shouts.

'Ya want me to lick ya boots clean, too?' Doug shouts back. 'I said I'm fuckin' sorry. Sorry, sorry, sorry, sorry,' he chants, until the word has no meaning any more.

'Don't get too clever, Doug, because I've had enough of you. You think you're King Billy the way you prance around.'

Jamie moves close to Doug, who retreats until he is backed into the wall.

'What's so fucking special about prison anyway, big shot?' yells Jamie, looming over him. 'You're the laziest, most ungrateful bastard that ever pissed on this earth. Got any witty remarks, you bloody little thief?' he shouts, his temper rising again and getting the better of him.

He raises an arm. Quick as a rat, Doug ducks and leaps for the table, grabbing up a knife. He spins and hunches into himself, fear of the huge man mirrored in his slitted eyes. His face is angry and his mouth sullen.

'Keep away from me, Jamie. I'll use it.'

Jamie looks at him with something akin to sorrow.

'What did I say only the other night, about you and your silly knives? What did I say I'd do, Doug?' he sighs. He shakes his head and moves in, confident of victory.

Doug tries to stab him, but he is effortlessly caught in a half nelson and his wrist is pinched until he drops the knife. Jamie kicks it away and breathes in Doug's ear.

'I'm sick of you, you poor little specimen. I'm going to squeeze you so hard that shit'll come out your ears. Try and stop me!'

He hurls Doug into the wall to fall to the cold safety of the floorboards. He is seized and held up in the air, while Jamie rains blows on to his unprotected head. Fists crash into his ribs and thin, sullen face. A left hook opens up his lip and loosens his teeth. A haymaker makes short work of his right eye and a power-house right fattens his ear and rings bells in his head. Jamie's hamlike fist connects with Doug's jaw, so he flies through the air and crashes into a chair, smashing it to smithereens. He rolls into the wall and waits for the boots.

But it is a soft body and the scent of soap and lavender that assails him. In his battered, bloody, state, he hears Jemima's screams.

A hand that is covered in blood, because splinters from the dying chair have torn into his palm, pats her shoulder to quieten her, but that is all Doug can muster his strength to do. Reassured, she stares in horror at the prowling Jamie, and knows that some-thing has gone from her life forever.

'You could have killed him, Jamie,' she whispers, awestruck at the violence around her.

'He pulled a knife on me — that's twice in two days, now. I'm not going to stand by while this mad jerk cuts up people at his every whim.'

'You could have killed my brother,' Jemima's wide eyes admonish him. For Jamie is the alien here, in front of this pale girl, covered in her brother's blood: with the blood of their father running through their veins.

'I wish he'd never bloody come down. He's just nothing but trouble, anyway. I should have killed him; someone should have smothered the crazy-eyed little prick the day he was born.'

'Screw you, ya 'Ighland git,' comes Doug's broken whisper from behind smashed lips, and Jamie moves towards him. But Jemima stamps her feet and screams, 'Shut up, the both of you! I've had enough. Just fuck off, Jamie. Haven't you done enough damage this morning? And as for you, Doug, you cunt!'

She has never been known to swear before, and this stops the two as much as her order.

'Go and cool down, Jamie. Please,' she says softly. 'I'll fix Doug.'

'He can clear out to his boong mates right away,' says Jamie viciously. 'I'll not have him on the place a moment longer than I can help it. And if I see him around, I'll bloody shoot him! You know what he's done? You can see what he's done, Jem. He's just destroyed everything sacred between you and me, like he's destroyed his Mum. Jesus Christ!'

'Go on away now, Jamie,' she murmurs and the blonde giant obeys her, hating the house and all it stands for. He drives out to the far pastures, and tries to salvage some joy there in the solitude, listening to the wind's wild poetry.

Back in the kitchen, Jemima gently bathes her battered brother and tries to patch up his bruised face as best she can, all the while soothing his mind and soul by humming some of Grandfather Tom's Irish songs. They are as sad and beautiful as she is now.

'You know, Jamie was most upset about your disappearance. He couldn't sleep last night for fear you were dead.'

'Well, 'e nearly succeeded in killin' me today,' Doug scowls.

'That's no way to talk to Jamie. It's your own fault for pulling a knife. Jamie doesn't like jokes like that.'

'I wasn't jokin',' Doug says.

'That's foolishness, Dougie. Jamie is my husband and I love him. So you would be stabbing me if you stabbed him. Would you do that to me?'

Their eyes lock for a long time, one pair gentle and the other wild with an unborn anger. Jemima has found her pleasures in life: if only he can, too, he will settle down and everything will be the way it should be.

A bandaged finger rubs her cheek.

''Course not. You all I got, my sister.'

'Well, you'd better go, Dougie. I'm sure Jamie will get over all this unpleasantness. But until he does, you'd do better to keep out of the way. You could hitch-hike back to Mum's.'

'Nuh,' he muses, 'I'll go over an' see Pretty Boy and Silver on Danny Jacobs' farm. There's sure to be fences needed fixin' there, he's such a lazy old bugger.' He tries to smile.

'Well . . . goodbye, darling.'

She kisses him on the cheek and, for just a moment, his eyes let her in on his soul. She feels that she has opened another Pandora's box, such misery and loneliness lurk there.

He collects his boots and coat from the Rover, picks up his scanty possessions and pats Tess cheerio.

He waves to the woman beside the door, then trudges off down the road.

What hurts him more than any of Jamie's hefty punches is that, when he went to say goodbye to his nephew, Willie, he encountered abhorrence and puzzlement in the child's eyes. That pained him so much that he will never forget it.

'Don't take it too hard — he's only frightened of the blood and bruises.' Jemima calls after the disappearing figure, but if he hears her he does not acknowledge it.

11

He does get a job at Danny Jacobs'. The old man needs help in sucker bashing and burning off, so Doug settles in with dark-eyed Floyd and dark-souled Silver. Once again the three are as they have always been, in their own tight, comfortable world with their private jokes and shared interests and memories that no-one can steal from them.

Every morning they roll out of bed and cook a feed, then the old man drives them out to the paddock on his cranky old tractor to clear the bush-ridden land.

Floyd drives the old Caterpillar bulldozer because he must always prove himself by being the best. Besides, his sharp brain and quick reflexes suit him for the difficult and sometimes dangerous job of operating the noisy, ponderous monster. Silver operates the chainsaw and Doug strips the logs of their branches and bark with an axe as he makes posts for fences and yards.

The youths revel in the hard work and in each other's company. They have not been together just by themselves for a long time. Amidst the tortured screams of the dying trees, as the chainsaw's teeth bite into the their virgin bodies, and the rumbling of the old faded red dozer smashing into the trees, knocking them senseless, and pushing them into broken piles, their raw yellow roots jagging obscenely into the air, and the thudding of the cruel axe, — amidst all this Doug no longer needs the friendship of the bush. In all its silent dignity it draws away from the youth who so badly needed a proper friend. Now he laughs as he slaughters the trees with his companions.

Pretty Boy, supreme upon the world's back and out of the way of Nylers and police, has lost his anger. His eyes sparkle as he laughs and talks of the car he will buy and the house he and Valerie will rent, all for themselves, when he goes back. Every night he lies back on the camp bed in the musty room the youths share and tells Doug all his plans and hopes. As soon as they save up enough money, he and Doug will leave for the delights of Perth and their two women. Silver may stay on with his mate, Shagger, who works as a storeman in the local town co-operative.

Old Danny Jacobs can best be described as red, white and blue; fat and happy. He has red skin, white hair and blue eyes. He is good to the three, neither working them hard nor letting them get away with too much slackness.

Doug forgets about the fence with which he was crowning the hill at Jamie's place. He forgets about dour Jamie McDonald and his sweet, soft sister and his trusting mother. Pretty Boy Floyd Davey understands him and loves him like a brother. Yellow fingers and black, laughing eyes beckon to Doug as surely as did the keys to Jamie's Rover and the grey, winding road.

At night the youths go out shooting the elusive kangaroos. They speed over the hills, Doug's competent hands on the wheel. The fleet, ghostly spirits that dart soundlessly across the ground are pinpointed in Silver's relentless spotlight and Floyd's dark eye behind that of the gun takes its toll.

They leap from the bucking ute and gather around the twitching forms with the anguished brown eyes that plead for the mercy they will never be given. A bullet in their brain will finish them, so their eyes glaze over, with still the glint of bewilderment in their liquid golden depths.

Is this the way to repay your earth mother: your whole being? A part of your heart lies bloody upon the ground.

Dancing, yelping Floyd and grinning Doug don't hear the earth groan and sigh in the blackness, as they cut off the tails and skin the warm quivering forms, then throw the unrecognisable carcasses into the back of the ute for the grunting pigs and slavering dogs to feed upon.

Sometimes they find a fox and then the fun begins. They pursue the cunning red streak, ducking and dodging between clumps of mossy old rocks and scarred old trees. Of course there are always the stupid rabbits that freeze in the bright glare of the car lights and wait, foolishly crouching, to die, leaping in the air with a woman's scream when they are shot.

Sometimes the youths borrow old Danny's ute and wander into town, to live it up in the small hotel or to go to the pictures. They live only for the shooting and the drinking and the invigorating work.

Then one Friday night, when they are engrossed in loud pop music from Doug's radio and a game of Jackpot (which Pretty Boy, with his sly fingers, is winning), there is a knock on the crumbling old door.

Shagger's red head peers around it, grinning cheekily. He ambles in with two flagons, for he knows how to get around these boys and he needs them now.

'G'day, fellers. Just dropped by to see youse.'

'Siddown 'ere, Shagger, an' try ya luck with the Pretty Boy,' Floyd calls.

They are all used to Shagger now. He is quiet and easy with his money, buying them drinks and anything they want. Besides, he has been almost everywhere, even to New Zealand and over east, so he can introduce new subjects into their conversations.

They play cards and drink and talk. There is to be a dance next week and Floyd promises to go there and rock the floor with all the local girls. Shearing is soon to start and they talk about various shearing feats. Shagger's shrewd green eyes flick about, waiting for the moment to spring his plan.

When Doug is slumped back, smiling dreamily and mumbling a song and when Floyd's slender fingers begin to fumble the cards while he cackles joyfully; the white man pulls his surprise.

'Now, tell me something, boys,' Shagger asks, 'how would you like to get five thousand dollars?'

' 'Ow'd ya mean, Shagger? What kind of job is that, anyways?' Pretty Boy mutters back, his dark eyes watching the freckled face.

'You know,' the redhead says mysteriously,' 'that shop in town where I work — on Friday — after the pig sale day on Thursday,' he leans closer towards the three, bringing them all into his exciting, wonderful world. 'It'll be easy. All I need is someone else to hold it up, because the old codger there knows me. I'll drive, though, no worries. Look, we'll be out and away before you know it.'

Floyd's eyes stare at Doug, who is only half listening anyway. As usual, the wine has sodden his brain.

Shagger concentrates on Floyd, because he knows he is the boss and the one who will ultimately make the decision. Silver already knows about the plan the big redhead has concocted while loading boxes and bags and unpacking cases out the back in the dusty old shed behind the co-op. Now it is up to Floyd, because Doug is nothing more than an easily influenced young drunk when it comes to the point. It's Pretty Boy who has the cunning and bravado that Shagger needs.

'Naw. Armed robbery ya talkin' about 'ere, Shagger. That's a wadgula style, that is. Ya wouldn't catch a nyoongah 'oldin' up places,' he says slowly.

'It'll be easy, Pretty Boy,' Silver replies, 'like Shagger says.'

'Just think of all the things that lovely moolah will buy you, mate,' wheedles Shagger. 'We're all mates 'ere, Floyd. No-one will dob anyone in. But we won't even be caught. Five thousand at least, and all you have to do is hold a gun and look tough. As easy as that. You can do that, surely?'

'Yeah.' Fingers shuffle cards uncertainly as Floyd thinks about it.

Shagger presses on to what he knows is Floyd's weak spot, his vanity.

'Go on! The way Silver used to talk about you, I thought you was tough; a man's man. Or else I never would have wasted my time. But it looks different from this side of the table.'

154

Shagger sees the fire light up in Floyd's eyes and presses his advantage. 'Listen, no-one has ever caught me yet, and I've done two robberies in my time. Me and Willie Nelson got away with eight thousand once, over east, and I broke into the Harvey post office last year and got away with a thousand dollars. That's form, Pretty Boy. That's Shagger Williams. Listen, you think you're hot as Huey, street fighting and doing shitty little breaks. That's nothing. Aaaaaahh!' He stands up and scoffs, playing his ace hand. 'The thing is you're too gutless to try the big time. You're all talk, Pretty Boy. All air. I sure am wasting my time here, Silver.'

He turns to go. Floyd leaps to his feet.

'Ya wanna bet, bub? Ya sayin' Pretty Boy Davey backed out of anything? This is Floyd Davey 'ere, ya white bastard, and I'll take ya on anytime. I'll 'elp ya rob ya poxy little store for ya, no fuckin' worries.' He snarls, with the drink inside him, for he cannot lose his pride; that is all he has.

'What about Dougo?' Shagger asks quietly.

' 'E's in on this too. This my brother 'ere, buddy, and where I go 'e goes, through thick and thin. Ya sayin' 'e's gutless too? I'll knock ya teeth in for ya, mate.'

'No. It's OK Floyd. Sit down while I tell you the plan.'

The situation has finally seeped through to Doug, past his wine heavy reveries.

'Nuh. No robbery for me. I only jus' got out of jail, look. I'm in all sort of shit, ya wouldn't believe, Shagger,' he mumbles. 'Tell 'im, Pretty Boy.'

'No, look 'ere, budda,' Floyd whispers, squatting down beside him. 'We need ya. Ya my best mate, Dougie, and I want ya to be in on this with me. All that boya will buy ya one good time with Polly,' he tempts. 'You and me could buy a car and take our womans anywhere we like.'

'All happy families,' beams Shagger.

'Happy days are here again,' sings Silver, so Doug smiles weakly and agrees. Why not? Everyone says there are no worries and Floyd will be right there beside him.

So the naked, fly-spotted bulb beams its cyclops eye upon the four and the shadows creep out to listen to their plan.

The idea is that Silver will stand guard at the door; Doug has the lesser job of backing up Floyd in the actual holdup. Silver will be covered in soot so he resembles an Aboriginal. After the robbery Shagger will drive to Perth and 'lose' the van. Silver, who has followed in the ute, will pick him up and drive straight back. Then Shagger will report the van as having been stolen from outside the pub and the blame for that and the robbery will be placed on three unknown Aboriginals.

The real culprits will have been clearing up all day if any questions are asked; who will know that they were not, for the short half hour the robbery will take?

The next day the sunshine gleams upon the dew-wet trees and grass, sparkling like jewels strewn by a rainbow all over the ground. The air is sharp and clear and warm; it is a buoyant day, bubbling with joy. Normally the youths tumble from the shed they camp in, rolling and shouting in play, on such a fine day as this.

But today they waken and see the empty chairs and empty flagons and the cards thrown carelessly over the scabby table. They remember last night and last night's words.

So Floyd moves slowly down into the yard with troubled downcast eyes and Doug follows behind despondently, his hands deep in his greatcoat pockets. Silver ambles behind, the only one who is happy, for he is too slow to realise the full potential danger this day might bring and only understands the excitement.

'We could always back out, ya know,' Doug mutters.

'Ya know we can't. What 'd everyone say if they 'eard? Big-mouth there would be sure to let them know.' Floyd jerks his heads backwards to where Silver whistles a cheery good morning to the birds.

'No, Doug,' he looks sadly into his friend's eyes, 'ya gotta do what ya gotta do in this life.' He half smiles. 'Keep old Danny busy while I get those guns.' He slinks into the house.

After a silent breakfast they set out to the clearing-up place where they are to wait until midday.

No-one does any work. They sit around, yarning and smoking and thinking.

This was going to be the night the three burned off. Danny has saved up some meat from the sheep he kills weekly and the boys have saved two rabbits and a piece of kangaroo meat. They were going to set fire to the dying heaps of wood they have bulldozed into piles, then have a barbecue in front of the last heap.

Once, just before Carey left his farm, Doug burnt off a huge swamp all by himself one night. Dragging kerosene-soaked rags on wire through the gently rustling reeds, he watched as the flames grew and towered, red raw and licking like snakes' tongues at the blue, star-spangled night. This light of his was far greater than the moon, and the hissing and pinging and roaring were far greater than the wind. The heat embraced him and he was like the grey ash people, floating serenely away.

He felt like someone then; it was wonderful to cause such a frighteningly beautiful sight as an entire swamp burning and dying as the ring of dancing advancing flames leaped and sprang. The fire was a magnificent, living thing that emphasised his loneliness and his power.

This night, tonight, will also be his night. Today will be his day, too; doesn't every dog have it's day?

At midday, they bump and scrape out to their prearranged meeting place, a shady grove owned by a tribe of slender white-gum saplings. There Shagger waits for them with his black panel van.

Doug and Pretty Boy share a nervous cigarette, while Silver rubs soot into his purple-red hair and over his freckled, pale face and arms. They get into the dungaree overalls Shagger has brought them while the white man reassures them.

'Don' worry about me, bub,' Floyd murmurs. 'Ya gotta worry before a thing like this. If ya don't, ya a fuckin' idiot. Somphin'll go wrong, then, if ya too cocky before'and.'

Doug just grunts when asked if he is all right and checks his double-barrelled shotgun with slim, confident fingers.

Up above, in one of the gently swaying trees, a magpie's soothing warble is heard. Doug scarcely hears the hymn.

'Nyaaah, nyaah, nyaah, ay-yah ah, ah, ay-yah, ay-yah, ay-yah,' chants Silver, leaping from behind the glossy black panel van. He claps his hands in a droning rythmn. A watery grin splits Pretty Boy's face at his friend's antics, while Shagger howls in glee and joins in the corroboree before crying, 'Let's go, boys.'

They pile into the panel van; Doug in the back, with the thick, rich, purple carpet. Out the small window he watches huge thick clouds coil up out of the horizon like a foreboding of doom. They are magnificent as they move across the sky. And the shapes they form: dragons and prancing centaurs, and witches and wizards, and all types of demons clashing in a battle of Armageddon proportions. They fade and die, reappearing in another terrifying shape; like harpies they swoop upon the charging black van. Rain, like blood, drips from the windows and from the weeping trees.

'Going to be a wet one,' Silver observes.

'Good. The streets will be empty and not so many witnesses around,' Shagger yelps happily.

Floyd just stares out the side window.

They reach the town at about four o'clock, when the sun has been dethroned and the demons rule the sky.

The Co-op stands, huge and white, on the street corner, the king of the buildings in this small town. The van cruises to a halt beside it and the keyed-up boys wait.

In the street is only a mongrel dog from the reserve, pissing unconcernedly against a white ant-eaten post.

Floyd turns and stares at Doug, who gazes back with eyes that Floyd has never seen before, murky and alert and soulful.

'Ya right, my brother? This won't take but a moment, ya know.'

Doug stares out at the cracked, empty town.

'A nyoongah's life is eatin', drinkin' and moonyin', ya told me once, Floyd. I dunno what the fuck we doin' 'ere,' he mumbles.

'Come on, Come on, let's get it over with,' hisses Silver in the middle, as taut as a violin string now that the moment has arrived.

Floyd's hand wraps around Doug's leg and he smiles.

' 'Ere I come, Polly Yarrup, with more boya than ya can 'andle.'

'Well,' Doug shrugs his shoulders, 'Dooligan the 'ooligan, actin' the fooligan.'

And the two chuckle softly as they pull old stockings across their faces.

Charge into the store.

Silver straddles the doorway and Pretty Boy leaps into the middle of the room, big and black and electric. Doug huddles near the icebox and wishes his knees would stop shaking.

'Don't fuck about. Just give us ya money, cunt!' shouts Pretty Boy. 'This is an 'old-up!' He shouts in his best TV drama voice.

The old man's mouth gapes open and he is stunned into immobility.

'Jesus,' he whispers.

But this is the Devil's day.

'Come on, don't fuck about! Do what 'e says,' cries Doug.

He feels powerful now: a veritable lord. He looks at the man's grey face and knows that he has caused the fear he sees there. It truly is his day. Everyone will remember this day with awe and wonder, and he is a part of it. He grins across at Floyd, who grins back. Doug turns to the icebox and helps himself to four small bottles of Coke in readiness for their victory toast in just a moment.

But no-one has thought of the old man's even older wife. She is short and dumpy, rather resembling one of the bags of flour her husband sells. She emerges now, with a shotgun pointed straight at Floyd's pounding, proud chest.

As Doug turns from the icebox he hears Floyd gasp and his eyes take in the scared woman in whose trembling hands a lethal weapon shakes.

Pointed straight at Pretty Boy who stares back, with wide eyes.

A few seconds pregnant stillness before violence is born.

Doug pulls the trigger of his gun and the right barrel spurts flame. Blood, as red as fire, spurts from the woman's chest and she crumples, coughing hideously.

The remnants of the blast hurry into the shadows. It echoes in Doug's brain, like a judge's gavel: like the footsteps of a sentenced man walking to the scaffold.

'Shit,' he whispers, 'Shit, she's dead,' he murmurs incredulously.

Everyone is still in a tableau of horror, but the old man recovers first. He plunges for his gun, still in the old woman's hands, and raises it, demented in fury, at a mesmerised Doug.

'Look out, brother,' Pretty Boy screams, and springs as the gun is fired. The bullets meant for Doug miss as he is sent sprawling into a stack of baked beans. The bullets decorate Floyd across the back and neck, in desert-red ochre, and the tall youth drops to the dusty floor.

Silver yells and fires wildly, causing the man to duck. Then he leaps forward and grabs a moaning Floyd, booting Doug out of his nightmare and back into today.

'Fuckin' get *out* of here! Christ! Someone help! Fuckin' Christ!' Silver chants now.

Doug and Silver drag their wounded companion out by the armpits while he howls all the time and they hurl him into the back of the van. At the sound of running footsteps, Doug spins around and fires his last barrel into the stomach of a charging constable, sending him somersaulting through the co-op window.

'Grab the mad bastard! What did he go berserk for? He's fucked up the whole lot,' yells Shagger, and Silver grabs Doug savagely, throwing him into the back beside Floyd's damaged body.

They speed out of town.

Confusion drowns Doug as the two white men shout together, Shagger trying to find out what went wrong and young Silver tearful at the catastrophe. The car shouts its own tune as it escapes the town.

Silver leans over and grabs thin Doug in one hand, wrenching him up. He presses his 22 into Doug's side and hisses like a viper, while Satan dances in his wild blue eyes.

'You little jerk! You killed Pretty Boy, you bastard. I'll fucking blow your fucking kidneys out, you cunt.'

'Huh,' Doug's dull eyes gaze blankly at Silver's face, his mind still in shock.

'Shut up.' Shagger belts Silver over the head so that he rolls moaning into the corner, tears rolling down his sooty cheeks.

This is the day on which they were going to be heroes.

'Listen carefully, now,' says Shagger calmly. 'We'll make for a hiding place and sort things out from there. Everythings going to be OK; no worries.' No-one believes him, not even himself.

They turn up an old track and grind along through the slippery clay and clinging mud until they reach a rickety old gate. They drive through and up onto a small tree-covered hill with a molasses-dark pool at the bottom. They park among the trees and climb out, exhausted mentally and physically.

Silver immediately grabs a listless Doug and throws him to the ground, booting him once or twice before Shagger's arms drag him off.

'Give over, Silver. That's not going to help. We're all in on this together now.'

'He killed Floyd,' Silver roars like the thunder.

'No, he didn't. No-one killed Floyd. Listen, go and get some wood and we can try and start a fire. I want to see how bad the poor bugger is hurt. Gawd spare me days, what a balls-up.'

'*He* ballsed it up,' rages Silver. 'He's simple. You know what he did, Shagger? We're up for murder now. That means hanging.'

'Get away, no-one 'll be hanged. No-one ever is,' Shagger mutters. 'Just get a fire going, Silver, that's all you have to worry about.'

Doug is picked up off the ground and patted kindly on the shoulder. Shagger shudders at the melancholy madness he sees in the youth's grey eyes, where before there had been only dreams.

Now it seems as though a great beast has emerged and stands in all its livery before the mouth of its cave.

Together they go to see how Floyd is.

Blood has soaked through the boy's fine silken shirt and has congealed upon the purple carpet, sticky and dark.

Can blood be so red? That's Pretty Boy's blood lying all over the place. He'll be dead soon. Doug ponders all this, detached and floating like a cloud.

'Hey, budda, can I get you a drink? Ya want a smoke, or somphin'?' he murmurs.

He is greeted only by a frightful howl that sends shivers down his back. He backs away, staring, paralysed by the Aboriginal's rolling eyes and blood-dribbling mouth. He looks like one of those kangaroos they shot the other night.

Doug wants to turn and run, unable to face reality. He vomits and retches dryly. That should be *him* lying there dying. If he lives to be a thousand he will never forget this day. His shaking arms encircle a slim, cool white tree, and he rubs his face against its pale trunk.

'Polly, Polly,' he whispers.

The wind is a whistling woman crying out to the Devil — her long purple hair flowing across the sky. She casts spells on the trees so they shamble like crooked gnomes around the bubbling cauldron of the pool.

His eyes stare into the water ruffled by the dribbling rain and he tries to bring back the dreams he had as a child beside a similar waterhole. But those days and dreams are gone forever.

He sees only his mother's eyes and hears his mother's words. Now he cries, as much for himself as for anyone else. He realises he is still holding the shotgun and hurls it, with a curse, far out into the pond. It falls with an ominous plop, mocking to the last, into a darkness as black as Floyd's eyes.

Doug stays there, he doesn't know how long. Only Shagger's calling stirs him from his woeful ruminations.

He makes his lonely way back to the van. Silver, crouched beside the little fire, ignores him. Shagger studiously watches the boiling water that leaps and froths in a battered can over the fire.

'We're taking old kid to the district hospital, then we'll piss off over east. That's all I can think of,' Shagger says as Doug comes out of the trees.

They creep out of their sanctuary and, like a rat, the van scurries down the highway.

Silence. No-one has anything to say.

Night slides down.

They crawl into the yard of the Katanning hospital at early dusk. Katanning is perhaps far enough away from today's incident to be ignored by the police patrols that are sure to be roaming the roads by now.

'You take the wheel, Dooligan. You're not to be trusted with a gun,' Silver commands. Doug obeys spiritlessly. Before he scrambles into the driver's seat, he touches Floyd's hand.

'See ya,' he says.

The hand is cold, as cold as death.

He knows then and hangs his head, biting his lips.

He hears a lot of shouting and looks up to see Shagger hustling two nurses through the rain, with Silver waving his rifle on the verandah in his best Charles Bronson manner.

One of the nurses is a half-caste who looks a little like Polly Yarrup. Doug remembers that Peringrup is down around here and wonders if she is a relative.

He gives her a tired smile; she is the nicest thing he has seen all day.

'It's been one fuckin' 'ard day, sis.'

Tremulous eyes gaze at him an instant before lowering to the task of taking out the dying, writhing Pretty Boy.

The nurses and the two white boys stagger back inside and Doug is left alone with his thoughts.

Thoughts of Floyd mostly: Floyd and he, drunk and laughing, arm in arm, in the black spaces and dead end streets of the Perth he loved best; Floyd angry and fighting, so alive; Floyd loving, in the Yarrup sisters' sleazy flat; Floyd talking the sense they could both understand, with his earnest eyes and gentle voice. They had some good yarns. He remembers Floyd hugging him and promising that they will be brothers for ever and ever and ever. And crying, both of them, though neither knew why.

He thinks of Tommy. He also killed people, but everyone praised him for that. Whereas he . . .

He thinks of jail.

This is the finish, Dougie, yet it's what you wanted really. Mum tried, Mr Salvadorez tried, Jemima and even Jamie tried, but look where you are now: on the dark side of the moon, he murmurs to the swishing windscreen wipers.

He cannot think of his mother. He thinks of Polly instead, her warm firm body and dusky musky smells, her darting, pink tongue and her eyes like cups of wine and the words of love that he drank like wine from them.

Valerie's face haunts him too.

Suddenly, through the driving rain, he sees three shadowy shapes crawl into the hospital yard; an RTA car, a police van and a CIB car, like a pack of hungry wary wolves. Doug sits still, like a fightened rabbit transfixed by their headlights.

Then he smashes a hand upon the horn so it blares out like a hurt cow and brings Silver skidding onto the verandah. He drops to his knee and lets off a shot at the confused huddle of cars, then hurtles down the steps as Shagger explodes through the hospital door.

A panic-stricken Doug has gunned the powerful motor as the police cars surge forward.

'Get out of here, Doug! Drive like the fucking wind!' yells Shagger as the two burst into the cab beside him.

Silver slams open the back door and pokes his gun out at the whining cars.

'Shoot them, Silver. We've got to get out of this!' Shagger cries, fear draining the blood from his face.

Down the road they swerve and twist and slide, the whole body of the great black creature trembling. Doug's the leader now. Shagger can curse and cry all he likes, Silver can fire angry rounds into the attacking demons, but Doug is the driver. It is his scrawny brown hands that control the delicate black wheel and his foot that keeps them just ahead of the maniacal trio.

This is Doug's moment.

He squeals out onto the highway on two wheels, while Silver yelps in fear and excitement and Shagger yelps in terror. A tiny smile floats onto Doug's lean face.

One of Silver's bullets shatters the window of the CIB car so that it swerves off into the darkness, but the other two charge relentlessly onwards.

Around a corner they swarm. An old sheep truck, as slow and as real as time, blocks the way. Doug swerves to pass.

Too late he sees the other car coming and tries to drop back.

The tortured shriek of metal on metal, as he slides along the side of the truck, and Shagger's screaming, high-pitched as a woman's, are the last things Doug hears before they cannon into the other car and disintegrate into flames.

Flames as high as those on the night that he murdered the swamp in readiness for progress and new crops. Flames as red as the blood of the dead killed on this fateful day. Smoke as black as Pretty Boy's eyes, billowing up to the cloudy ghosts that wander around the sky after today's battle. All in a silence as quiet as Doug Dooligan's many dreams.

BCID: 806-7609798

www.bookcrossing.com

Glossary

boya	money
budjarrie	pregnant
bunji	'to bunji around' is to go from person to person, conning them up and so forth. A bunji (man or woman) makes love to anyone.
gabba	wine; literally 'blood'
gunyah	bush hut
guritch	good
koomph	urine; urinate
mardong	when someone really loves you and wants to go with you
monaych	police; literally, 'the man with chains'
moony	sexual intercourse
nummery	cigarette
nyoongah	originally the Bibbulmum people of the south-west but nowadays any part-Aboriginal person
orga or yorga	women
tuppy	vagina

unna	'Isn't that so/' or 'Is that the truth?'
wadgula	white people
winyan	not altogether there in the head
wongi	really the people from Kalgoorlie way, but any full-blood Aboriginal
woodarchi	evil spirits; small hairy men with red eyes, some say; or else a featherfoot
yorrn	an expression of sorrow